## Praise for Donna Hemans's Extraordinary Debut Novel

"The power and the language of *RIVER WOMAN,* and the irresistible call of the story, and thanksgiving in the prese *RIVER WOMAN* is the work you don't want to break an forget."

—Marita Golden, author of *The Edge of Heaven*

"The minute I read the first couple of pages, I was hooked. Donna Hemans is a talented writer."

—Elizabeth Nunez, author of *Bruised Hibiscus*

"[A] potent, accomplished debut. . . . Will Sonya come to her daughter's defense or abandon her again? Hemans pitches the question as intensely as a thriller writer and answers it as resonantly as a poet."

—*Publishers Weekly*

"Like the works of Edwidge Danticat and Jamaica Kincaid, Hemans' first novel is one of stark lyricism and shattering emotional honesty."

—*Library Journal*

# River Woman

## Donna Hemans

WASHINGTON SQUARE PRESS

New York   London   Toronto   Sydney   Singapore

**WSP**

A Washington Square Press Publication
1230 Avenue of the Americas, New York, NY 10020

Copyright © 2002 by Donna Hemans

Originally published in hardcover in 2002 by Washington Square Press

ISBN: 0-7434-1040-8

First Washington Square Press trade paperback printing January 2003

10  9  8  7  6  5  4  3  2  1

WASHINGTON SQUARE PRESS and colophon are
registered trademarks of Simon & Schuster, Inc.

For information regarding special discounts for bulk purchases,
please contact Simon & Schuster Special Sales at 1-800-456-6798 or
business@simonandschuster.com

Printed in the U.S.A.

*for my parents,*
**Norma and Charles,**

*and my sisters,*
**Calaine and Judy**

# Acknowledgments

Gratitude and thanks:

To my editor, Tracy Sherrod, for her astute comments and editorial guidance, and to my agent, Lynn Whittaker, for believing in the promise of a young writer.

To my peers and colleagues at American University's Creative Writing Program who read early drafts of this and other works, and to my writing instructors, especially Richard McCann, Kermit Moyer, and Myra Sklarew, who gave early guidance on a draft submitted as my MFA thesis.

To my parents, Norma and Charles, and my sisters, Calaine and Judy, for answering my e-mail and telephone queries and for providing immeasurable support.

# The Drowning

Women around me were screaming, running, and somebody was shouting, trying to get my attention. They'd left their clothes upon the rocks where they were beating out the yellow stains that their husbands' sweat had left in the armpits of the shirts. Soapsuds were still on their arms.

I could hear the pitter-patter of their feet on the gravel that had been washed over thousands of times by the river, or covered completely when heavy rains swelled the river and made it impossible for us women to gather there.

I saw when Pam hiked her skirt above her thick, scarred knees and kicked off her broken-down sneakers, so she could run faster. The other woman, whose baby always had one hand in her mouth and the other wrapped in her mama's skirt, violently shook the infant's hands away. I saw Carol's breasts swinging from side to side underneath her red T-shirt. Her dark nipples protruded because the water from washing had flattened her T-shirt against her body. I wondered if her breasts didn't hurt from flapping like that against her stomach.

It wasn't till I saw Pam grab the small body in the blue shirt, which had a hole in the front, that I noticed my baby was missing from under the tree where I had left him sleeping.

"Mi baby, mi baby! Oh, mi God, mi baby!" I cried, pushing my way between the women who were pulling my boy's body out of the water. "Timothy, Timothy."

The women, all mothers themselves and much older than I was, wouldn't let me near my baby's soft body, which they had placed on the sand. Pam, although I'm sure she'd never done anything like this before, pressed her mouth, her chapped lips, against my baby's pink lips and tried to force some of her air into his lungs. But his little three-year-old body didn't move, couldn't move. Another woman tried to press his chest and force his heart to beat again.

"Hol' 'im upside down and let the water out," someone I couldn't see shouted from behind.

My baby, Timothy, who squealed each time I bathed him and didn't play in the water like most babies like to do, had awakened, left the shade tree where I had put him to sleep, walked to the bank of the river, and drowned in water that was scarcely high enough to wet my skirt.

All river women, and not one of us knew how to save a drowning boy.

They pressed his chest. They blew air into his mouth. Mattie pressed her ear against his chest and said she heard no beats. Someone prayed. Another woman cried.

They looked at me as if I were the river and not the mother. They wouldn't let me touch him. They didn't want to accept that my baby had walked into the water when I wasn't looking and drowned. The river had filled his little lungs with water and smothered the air he was trying to push in and out of his body.

I pushed away the women who were holding me back.

I simply wanted to hold his soft body in my arms one more time before it began to stiffen.

They asked me what I saw, what I heard. They were impatient, like roosters trying to get at hens. Someone said the word "police."

I don't know how it happened. The current wasn't really strong. I hadn't yet lost any sheets, nor any of Timothy's or Grams's clothes. The current wasn't strong.

"You didn't see de bwoy walking to you? You never see him when he fall into de water?" they asked, but I know I didn't see my boy's head bob back up to the top of the water, or hear the gurgle deep in his throat when he tried to say "Mama" and swallowed water instead. I didn't see his arms, in the little blue T-shirt, reach out in the air and then drop back down beneath the surface of the water. Nor did I see the water push his body, facedown, into the soft gray sand on the bank of the river before pulling him out again, and then depositing him again. I didn't see the ripples in the water or the air bubbles his breath formed in the water. I didn't see him drown.

While I was rocking my baby one last time, I heard another woman say she was going to the main road to flag down a car, since the one ambulance wouldn't come out here to pick up the body of a dead boy.

3

I held him. His body was limp in my arms, not yet rigid but stiffening slightly. There was nothing in his face, nothing in the eyes that somebody had closed, but which I opened slightly with my fingers. The water from his clothes dripped down my arms, streaking and tickling, mingling with the soapy water on my body. I fell to the ground, the sand and the rocks hard against my legs and bottom. Timothy lay in my arms, his head rolled back as if he were just looking at my face, as if he had been looking at me and fallen asleep with my face printed on his mind. My salt water mingled with his river water. I whispered the name "Mommy Kelithe," the way he said it, as if one name was never enough.

I held his body tight, and when the car came, somebody led me to it. I remember Timothy's body, soft and wet against my chest, and the tickling of water from my eyes rolling over my cheeks, falling gently on the wet body of my son.

This is what I would have told my mother, if only she had asked.

# Fairy Tales

~

Brown bugs bring news. Good news if they hover or land. Bad, if they fly away. Sonya stretched out her hands for what should be a light touch, a feeling like the kiss of a butterfly, the waiting made comfortable by the song of the brown bug's wings. She would have waited for hours for the news of good news to come, except the baby dropped an empty bottle by her feet. Except the baby looked into her empty eyes with a plea for more. Except. Except. Except.

And it wasn't really a brown bug anyway. Not the light brown news bug from back home. This was simply a brown bug, a foreign bug, that hovered near the rose bushes on the balcony of her employers' Manhattan condo. She wanted good news from somewhere, whether from a bug that didn't carry news or whether falling from the sky like rain. So she fixed her mind on the end, always the end, the way she did when she told stories to the children she watched by day. Goldilocks always ran away from the three bears first. And then she worked back, back, back, till she came to tell Goldilocks's mistake of entering the house and eating porridge that wasn't hers. The three little pigs always built the brick house first and laughed at the wolf huffing and puffing away. It was only after she told the children of the pigs' success in getting away from the wolf that she told them of the two narrow escapes and the pigs' fright when the straw and stick houses fell down.

Sonya thought like that now, dreaming of the good news, putting off till later the worries that had driven her from inside the cool house, away from the lemon scent of Endust, the children's unending desire to help smooth the little blue cloth across the dark wood furniture, their soft, tiny fingers pressed against hers. Then, too, there were the clothes she had left in the drier too long, which now needed to be pressed and folded, and the master bathroom to clean, and the steaks that she liked to cook until they were brown but which the man and lady of the house preferred to eat with a little bit of pink inside. There was little time to sit outside waiting for something that probably wouldn't come.

For a long time she had made good news her focus. Long before she left her five-year-old daughter back home with her mother and long before she searched but couldn't find a way to explain to such a small child how to not think about the now or the waiting but to think instead of the happy ending when she would come live with her mother in a faraway place over the seas; a place that wasn't heaven or hell because her mother wasn't dead or dying, but just going away to another country for a while. She had wanted to give her daughter a story, a happy ending like the ones she had dreamed over and over again throughout her youth. But the happy endings she thought of didn't sound appropriate for her daughter when she turned them over in her mind, perhaps because she was thinking so much about the happiness to come for herself in that other place, which she imagined to be something like Kingston, only better and not hot all the time.

When she was younger, one of the endings she liked to envision had her standing at the top of the metal steps of a plane and letting her straw hat loose. The wind would pick up the hat, and it would float like a hummingbird, swooping and fluttering in one place for a while before it lifted again and sailed away from her. She would turn her back, then, and imagine her parents on the waving gallery catching it, her final farewell to them.

Back then her leaving was still only a dream—good news to come—and one that had shifted shapes from time to time. Sometimes she simply dreamt of leaving Standfast on a bus, standing on the top where people loaded bags and boxes, and looking back on the town, waving good-bye forever. In other dreams, she worked at a hotel in Ocho Rios or Runaway Bay, making beds and cleaning rooms—a short daytime or weekly escape—but an escape nevertheless from the dirt roads of Standfast and the dust that always blew through the windows, coating everything with a thin film. When she got pregnant, she imagined her baby's father taking her away on his motorbike. In that dream she sat behind him, her rounded stomach pressed against his back, one hand holding her skirt down against the breeze and her other arm wrapped around his waist. And sometimes in her dreams a veil rose in the breeze and floated behind her like a low-flying kite. She never knew where that dream came from, for marriage was never a consideration, not on his part anyway; he didn't even stay around when her father picked up a stick to beat the man who had gotten his daughter pregnant.

Those weren't the kinds of story endings that a five-year-old could understand.

When Sonya left Standfast, her departure didn't happen like any of those in her dreams. Her baby's father was long gone, afraid of an old man with a stick. There was no one on the waving gallery at the airport. She wasn't so worried about leaving her mother behind, but she was concerned about the daughter who would recognize her mother's handwriting better than she recognized her face. She had no straw hat, but had curled her straightened hair so it covered her ears and neck and tiny bangs floated over her forehead. She worried about the curls in her hair dying when humidity and sweat took hold. Sonya worried, too, about the smell of the fried fish, wrapped in foil and settled in the bottom of her handbag. She kissed her mother, patted her daughter's head, and turned away to the blue-tinted glass. Through the glass she saw her daughter's face pressed into her mother's skirt and heard the question, "When Mommy coming back, Mama?" Sonya wanted to go back and hug her daughter, but the immigration official wouldn't let her through. She could only think then of the comforting soon-soon words she had left her daughter with. But those words weren't the words of a happy ending, more like the kind of words that would leave a baby bird's mouth hanging open in wait for its mother's return.

When she turned away that day from her daughter and walked away behind the blue glass, she had sat on a couch for a little while crying because she couldn't get the image of the bird's open mouth out of her mind. She saw her daughter waiting and waiting, standing by the gate to the yard, her eyes fixed on something to come, but never, never knowing when her good news—her mother—would arrive.

Sonya's own waiting for good news was different, because no one had promised her anything. Not her baby's father, nor her own mother or father. Her parents, especially, had simply taken things as they came. "One day at a time," they always said. She wondered if her mother would say the same now to Kelithe, to soothe her anxiety by singing the words of the song: "One day at a time, Sweet Jesus / Tomorrow may never be mine. . . ."

And now, once again, Sonya couldn't think of a fitting end. No good news to replace the bad news of the night before. Three phone calls, one message. The grandson she knew only by the size and shape of his footprint on paper, the size of his clothes, an out-of-focus Polaroid, bubbly laughter in the background of telephone conversations, was dead. Accidentally drowned, one caller said. "Kelithe watch him drown," another said. "You' gran'son drown and Kelithe heart broken," her own mother said.

She would have preferred no news at all. Or simply a prolonging of the good news of three weeks ago—finally having the money and the space and the papers to send for her daughter and to fulfill a fifteen-year-old promise. And her husband's word that the time was right for her now-adult daughter to come live with them. She would have preferred almost any-

9

thing to the tickling, unanswerable question: Did Kelithe watch?

"Your papers came through. I ready to sen' for you now." She let the three-week-old words roll off her tongue and wished she could swirl them around her mouth the way she swirled water or ice cubes on a hot day. She wanted to remember forever the feeling of the words filling her mouth, falling from her lips, the feeling of imagining her daughter's happiness at finally leaving Standfast for a foreign place. But no good news would come, and even the memory of the good news of three weeks ago was not enough to erase the question she didn't want to ask.

Sonya handed a fresh bottle to the baby, and when she looked down at his lips greedily sucking the bottle, his fingers gripping the bunny-shaped plastic, she thought how easy it was to make him happy. She struggled to bring an image of Timothy to mind and closed her eyes to sharpen the memory of a photograph. She thought about it as if she were trying to make out images on an unfocused television screen. Her eyes were narrowed and her brows wrinkled. She saw Kelithe's face first, the chubby, red, wrinkled face of a newborn baby, and tried harder to remember the features she had seen in the underdeveloped Polaroid shot of her grandson. Kelithe at one, standing at the door to the kitchen and looking back to hear the words she knew would come: "Don't go in there." Kelithe at two, in Grams's room, bottles and books from the dresser scattered on the floor and a guilty look splayed across Kelithe's face. Kelithe at three, starting school and wearing a red-and-white plaid uniform, with red bows in her hair. The images of Kelithe were sharp photos in an album.

But her grandson's face she couldn't see. She remembered,

though, the pieces of clothes she had bought for him, or collected from neighbors, and the very early layette sets that she had used for her secondborn and packed in a barrel to send home for her grandchild. If she had known the father of the child, she thought, perhaps she could blend his face with Kelithe's to conjure up how Timothy looked. But she didn't know the baby's father, and she thought now that perhaps Kelithe, herself, didn't know.

The lull of the river came to her mind, too, and the women, their backs to the road, soapsuds on their arms, feet spread, bottoms high in the air, backs bent. Sonya pictured clothes spread on the banks of the river and across shrubs. Women, so many women. She heard their voices, the squish-squish of water and soap and cloth, the sound of the water moving downstream. She pictured Kelithe folding the baby clothes she had packed and sent, and then picking up her basin and soap and catching her baby's hand. In her mind-picture, mother and son walked up the bank of the river, the talkative three-year-old singing a song his mother didn't know and skipping over the loose stones. Only, the baby in her thoughts looked like a darker version of the boy at her side.

It was as if someone had opened a bottle and released the odor of the river, the smell of wet, decaying leaves, a rawness not quite like that of fish but a smell not far from it either. She felt too the slippery leaves beneath her feet, the polished feel of river stones washed over and over. It was a long time since she had washed clothes by the river, and the freshness of the memory surprised her.

"Not like I want to go back and do that. Don't know why I thinking 'bout that now."

Still, the thought of mother and son walking home from the river was the closest Sonya could come to a good end, a happy end. But it didn't replace or erase the questions. It was only now that she was rethinking the phone calls that she realized she hadn't asked the callers the why or the how that should have come after the news of the baby's death and, even more naturally, after the accusation that her daughter had stood by and watched. Because she couldn't fill in the because, her questions hung in her mind, making her hate herself for thinking such thoughts about her own daughter, for thinking that Kelithe could have watched her son walk into the river and not done anything to help him out. And even though she regretted not having asked her callers all her questions, she was a little happier because not knowing left some room for hope.

"She could never do that." It was only when the little girl said, "What, Nanna?" that she realized she had spoken out loud.

"Who could never do what?"

"Nothing. Nothing."

"I could never do it? Were you talking about me?"

She had forgotten the persistence of the four-year-old girl, forgotten that if she didn't get a full answer, she made up answers and spoke them aloud until she hit on one that satisfied her or until the person to whom she had directed the question gave her a satisfactory reply.

"You want some strawberries?" Sonya asked instead.

"Strawberries. Strawberries."

Sonya listened to the strawberry song that followed her from the room. The baby, too, was trying to sing the words his sister sang.

With the strawberry song at the back of her mind, she went back to work and thought about making some plans to help bury her grandson and bring back her now-adult daughter, whom she had told years and years ago, "Soon, soon you'll come live with me. Nex' year, when things get better." The years stretched, and it wasn't until ten years later, when her then-fifteen-year-old daughter turned up pregnant at a boarding school, that she'd gone back to Jamaica and seen how her daughter's five-year-old face had really changed and could tell what she would look like as a woman.

Ten years without hearing the word "Mommy" from her firstborn. It was a different feeling when her secondborn said, "Mommy," or when the two children she looked after during the days accidentally called the dark-skinned woman who could never be their mother Mommy. When her secondborn called her Mommy for the first time, she felt warm, yes, but she didn't get the full-heart feeling of hearing her new name for the first time, and thinking of the role she would play for the rest of her life.

"Mommy." The one-year-old dropped his bottle again and held out his hands to her.

Sonya went toward him. She didn't want to pick him up, but she let him wrap his arms around her legs instead. She thought briefly about her grandson's now-stiff arms, which she would never feel wrapped around her legs.

Although she never watched the sun, she thought of it dragging across the sky. She wanted to get back outside, to feel a breeze or to look for the news bug again. She would have settled for anything to take the baby off her mind and relieve the guilt that she thought she wouldn't be feeling if she had only spoken to her daughter after hearing that her grandson had died. But conversations with Kelithe made her feel like somebody had drilled a hole in her body and left it open for the wind to blow straight through from back to front.

"Hello, Ma, is me, Kelithe." Sonya remembered the three-week-old conversation.

"Yeah, how's everything? Mama all right?"

"Yes, everything all right. I got your letter."

Kelithe always went straight to the point of her call. And her words were sort of formal, as if she were talking to a person she had only just met and not to her own mother. The conversation came back to Sonya slowly. The only part of the conversation she had savored and banked in her memory was the part where she said she was ready for her daughter to come live with her. But the earlier happy parts that came when her husband said, Yes, it was okay for his now-adult stepdaughter to come live with them, she didn't, couldn't, share with Kelithe. Sonya was ashamed to let her daughter know that the man she had married had been the one preventing her daughter's arrival all these years. He hadn't been ready for Kris, the daughter they had together, either, but he had accepted her the way her own mother had accepted Kelithe when she was born.

So many times over the years she had wanted to start the paperwork to bring her daughter "home." And each time her husband, Anthony, held up the checkbook and pointed out the amount left over after food and gas and electricity and rent and subway money and the car payment and insurance and the telephone and things for Kris had all been paid for.

"It don't make sense to bring her out of that to this," he said all the time. But he didn't know Standfast, and Sonya

14

didn't want to explain about the place she had spent her youth longing to escape. Instead she said yes, because she had never really been ready for motherhood. And she could relay her husband's words to her own mother and let the full blame for Kelithe's prolonged stay in Jamaica rest entirely on his shoulders, without her own mother ever suspecting that all those years later Sonya was still not ready to accept completely her role of mother.

When Sonya was finally ready to do it alone, her mother had sent a telegram to say Kelithe's school had sent a telegram and left a phone message at the post office to say that Kelithe was pregnant and couldn't take classes anymore and that her parents or guardian or somebody should come take the child home because they wouldn't put a pregnant teenager on the bus alone because she might run away and not go home at all. Sonya had been ready, finally ready, to defy her husband and accept her mother's word that a child belonged with its mother. But how could she take care of her own fifteen-year-old daughter, her four-year-old daughter, and her first daughter's baby? She had gone to Jamaica instead, removed her showing-already daughter from the school, and taken her back to Standfast, the place where she had left her ten years before with a promise.

"Yes, I ready for you to come now. I goin' sen' the papers and the ticket to you." Those were the magic words, the words she knew her daughter had waited year after year to hear. Fifteen years of waiting. But the hooray Sonya expected to hear came out only as a weak, "Yes, ma'am." There was no screech of happiness, no prolonged thank-you, no breathless excitement.

"But you have to leave the baby for now. . . ."

The children screamed before Sonya realized she had dropped a glass. "You have to leave the baby for now. Could that—" She closed her eyes to stop herself from thinking that her "You have to leave the baby for now" could have made her daughter watch her baby drown. She knew it wasn't the answer. She didn't want that to be the answer, for the memory of those words put more distance between the answers to the questions that surfaced after Sonya's callers said Kelithe had stood and watched the baby drown.

It wasn't till she heard the second scream that she realized the baby had walked into the kitchen. He was sitting on the floor, looking at the blood flowing from his foot where a piece of glass had cut him.

"No, no. Don't come in here, girl. Stay right there." She ran to the bathroom with the baby, grateful for a distraction.

# Country Women's Ways

On Saturday, on my way to view Timothy's body, a child throws a stone at me. It bounces on other rocks and lands near my feet. "Chew," Timothy would have said. A perfect imitation of the sound of the stone. "Chew."

"Mind what you doing, boy," I wanted to say, would have said at another time.

The boy, a little bigger than Timothy, doesn't even run when I turn to look. Last week, he, Timothy, and I stood side by side and sucked frozen orange suck-suck we bought from the ice-cream man. The boy's thirst was bigger than mine. When he finished his bag of flavored ice, his mouth still watered, and he looked with want at Timothy's half-finished one. I dropped coins in his palm, and he ran through the dust to the ice-cream man's motorbike.

"Watch me an' you," another child shouts. "I goin' tell you' mother say you a throw stone."

"She not goin' say nothin'. She say that girl, Kelithe, is the devil own chile. She watch her son drown."

Talk follows me everywhere I go. Low whispers. Loud voices. Soft, understanding, forgiving, harsh, gentle, critical, voices follow me, walking with me as I first walk through Standfast market among the wooden stalls. Grams wanted scallion and cabbage, and I wanted to get them before the sun wilted their freshness. People step aside when I come near. "Back up, back up there," they say to each other, and all take a few steps back.

But nobody says anything to me directly.

Country women don't whisper behind their hands when they are badmouthing you. Country women talk out loud whether you are right there in front of them or miles away, and you hear of the talk because someone else brings the news back to you. Country women don't hold anything back the way the city women do. No, country women aren't like the city women who sit in the Anglican or Catholic or Methodist churches yawning behind their fans on Sundays, their wide hats covering their eyes, hiding their thoughts. The ones who would never set foot in one of our clap-hand Baptist or Pentecostal churches, the ones who used to shake their heads when someone caught the spirit at the church we used to go to when I went away from here to school. No. Those women used to look back when someone jumped up with the spirit or clapped or shouted out loud in church. The ones in Orange Valley who turn their heads because my sneakers are bent down in the back and my heels are dragging in the dirt. The ones who talk about other people and hug or shake their hands when next they meet, asking sweetly how everything is and pretending to be shocked when they hear the person's tragic news.

Like it was when I saw Marissa, a girl who was in school with me and who graduated two years before I would have. She looked me up and down, looked at my shoes, and whispered something to the woman who was next to her, her mother probably.

"Kelithe?"

I looked at her for a little while, wanting to pretend to be someone else, Kelithe's sister maybe.

"Yes. You look like somebody I know."

"From school. You remember me, Marissa, from school."

"Oh, yes. I see the resemblance now."

"So what you doing out this way?" Her eyes scanned my clothes and hair and shoes again and the baby at my side.

"Just back home now. This is my son, Timothy."

"Oh. I didn't know you had a baby. . . ."

I knew she must have known I hadn't finished school, must have heard the whispers about me from others who had graduated or others who were still there. I looked her straight in the eye, wanting her to ask. But she looked off into the distance, squinting against the sun. When she looked back at me, she said it was time for her to go. She looked down at Timothy, too, and when she walked off, I saw her head shaking from side to side.

No, country women aren't like Marissa. Standfast women aren't like Marissa. They talk and let you know they are talking. They never approach you. They just talk, and you know they are watching and waiting for you to do something, anything, to give them something else to talk about, some other piece of news to carry on to someone else.

*"She know she was getting them papers to go a foreign. And she never had nothin' to do wid the baby since her mother tell her that she couldn't tek the baby wid her to New York. At least not yet anyways. And the Grams too old to tek on a pickney that young. I believe she knew that baby was in the water and she watch him drown to get her chance to go a foreign."*

*"Bet the Grams believe is the devil work."*

*"Obeah! If she was down there the day to see it wid her own eye she wouldn't think like that."*

*"See her over de across the street . . . the devil own self, the gal Kelithe. Come back thinking she better than everybody 'cause she go off to high school. Talking like she better than everybody. But no better. Pregnant wid no father for the baby. And now she kill the chile. Better if she never did mek him born in this world. A wicked woman, I tell you."*

*"That's what the worl' coming to."*

Nobody accuses me. But I know they are thinking that I watched my child drown because I wanted to be free to leave this deep-country town. But I can't do anything about the anger that burns in their eyes like a red roaring fire. I can't break down and cry. I can't fall on my knees and beg to be forgiven for the wrong they accuse me of doing.

What can I say?

Grams used to say that a hen loses to a rooster because it fights too hard. Hens flap their wings, squawk loudly. The

20

rooster stands, its beak at the hen's neck. He waits till she is out of breath. He wins. A simple strategy. Don't fight back too hard, she said. She used to say, as well, that if I talk too loudly, am too quick to defend myself, it shows that I'm guilty. But people also say that a silent river runs deep.

They want me to cry and kick and scream. My grief is my own. Not theirs.

The whispering follows me when I leave the market. The trip takes a long while because I don't go by the clearing at the river where the women gather to wash. I expect they will be there. Mostly, I don't want to see the place where Timothy went down. Now, I catch rainwater in a drum outside the house, sun the clothes on sheets of zinc, and wash in the yard by the side of the house, hidden from the street and passersby who want to look over the hedge. From there, I can't hear the bitter words and see the angry stares from the women by the river. Their words drain me of my will to live.

I notice all the sounds Timothy would have noticed: the Rio Minho's *shhh-shhh;* a donkey's hee-haw; a dove's sad cry; the rustle of the breeze against my plastic bag. In the bus, I count the bamboo trees he used to point out and count. The poinciana trees with flowers like flames. Sometimes he would count croton trees because Grams told him once that wherever he saw a croton tree, it meant a body was buried there. She told me the same thing when I was little so I wouldn't be scared of the dead. I wasn't. There were too many croton trees around. Now she tells me not be afraid of the living, the women who crowd around me and shout their nasty words.

I take my time getting there. I'm not anxious to see Timothy's body without life. By the time of the funeral he will look a

21

little bit more like himself. I catch a glimpse of myself in the window of Pear's Haberdashery. A green T-shirt with a compass on the front. A skirt that I remember used to be black. No smile. Sad eyes. I lift my cheeks to make a plastic smile. My eyes are still sad. I practice smiling until I see Mrs. Chen looking back out at me.

"Shoo." I imagine that's what she mouths.

Nobody here knows me. And it makes me a little less sad. No one stares when I walk. No one backs away as if I have TB or whispers loudly behind a cupped hand. I don't listen for whispers or have to imagine the answers I would give if somebody approached me. When leaves and branches sway in the breeze, I don't look twice to see if there is a face hidden or a brown body trying to blend in with the brown tree trunk. I could have taken the bus all the way here. But I chose to walk for the very reason that no one knows me, that I won't see fingers point my way or have to dodge words the way I would run away from stones.

I take my time getting there. Orange Valley Funeral Home with the statue of the Virgin Mary holding her son, her head bent and eyes focused on the stone face of the baby. Mother and son should not have been made of stone but molded out of flexible plastic like that of a doll. Softness. That's what grieving mothers want.

The women must have known where I was going. Although they didn't follow me, they are there ahead of me, blocking the steps and the entrance, the name "Orange Valley Funeral Home," the statue of the Virgin Mary and her son. There are nine of them. They seem to move as one, shifting to the door at the side when I move to the left. They're all a few years older than me, probably none older than thirty. I'm glad it is daylight. If it had been night—though I don't believe in spirits—I surely would have thought this group of women represented a set of spirits come to haunt me. I look at their hands first. No stones, but tightly folded fists.

I don't know what they want. It can't be Timothy's body. What would they do with it? If they want me to know they haven't forgotten, they didn't have to do this. How can I forget when bodies back-back away from me, and hands don't cover mouths when they say my name?

Now I know what it means for time to stand still. Eighteen eyes staring at me. Nine chests rising and falling, pushing out breaths as heavy as if the owners had been running or were the winners of a vicious fight.

I think of a childhood game, a way to prepare myself to run or fight. To myself I sing, "Bull in a pen, can't come out," and gear myself up to charge, as I would in the game at the hands forming the circle around me. It's the same song I used to sing when I played netball at school. The song made me an aggressive player, the one always chosen to play defense at the hoop.

Bull in a pen, can't come out. That's the way I feel. Like a thick sheet or heavy tarpaulin is closing in over my head. Bull in a pen.

"What's going on?" A man's voice comes through a window. "Don't bring your trouble over here."

His black suit fills the doorway. And I'm happy for the distant presence.

23

"Move on, or I'll call the police." His eyes seem to fall on each face. He finally looks at me, and I hope he recognizes me. "You have a choice, the police or the dogs out back. Move on."

One by one the women walk by, a hearse the only thing between them and me. The last woman, Lisette, backs away, her eyes, red as if she'd been crying, never leaving my face. When she backs up to the gate, she faces the other women and turns around once, twice, to look at me again. I imagine her as a schoolgirl bully, saying, "I not finish with you yet. Wait till school over." All these years, and the menace was still in her eyes.

"What they want?" the man asks when I get to the top of the steps.

"They all obeah women. They want to work some magic on his body."

He laughs, a sound both loud and soft, a little like the scratching of a branch against a zinc roof. I wish I could do the same.

Inside, the walls are bare. I want to see some pictures, perhaps flowers, even though the reds and greens and yellows are certain to look nothing like the colors of real flowers growing outside. We step into his office first, and he offers me a glass of ice water. I drink without stopping, aware now how scared I was of the women I had known all my life. Everything in the office seems to be made of wood. There is no clutter of paper. The office is as empty as if it is used only for meetings like these with grieving families.

Nothing here seems real. Not dead—simply without life. Mr. Gordon, when he stretches out his hand and introduces himself, also seems like a body without life. His voice is soft, the direct opposite of the sound that was thrown at the women outside. That voice chased nine women away. This one must be his grieving family voice.

When I've finished the water and settled the glass on the table, he asks if I want to see my son's body. At first I shake my head no, something I was told over and over was not polite.

"It always helps the family to look at the body," he says, as if he and I are sharing a secret. "Viewing brings closure."

Again, I say no. "He's not fixed up yet, is he?"

"No. Not yet. By Thursday, maybe. But we still need you to identify the body. It's our policy. Someone has to look and say, 'Yes, this is so and so's body.'"

Mr. Gordon reminds me of someone from long ago. The school guidance counselor. She spoke as softly as he did, and all the girls said, "She must think me and she are friends." Then, I didn't like that conspiratorial whisper. And I don't like it now.

"Okay."

He leaves me in the room and walks down the hall by himself. My throat is closing in again, and my lips are burning from dryness. When he returns, I tiptoe behind him, trying to quiet my footsteps falling on the shiny, wooden floor. The walk reminds me of another one long ago. I am in the back, and the nurse and guidance counselor are in front. The hallway is empty. Their shoes clap against the floor, and it reminds me of the sound of a leather belt or ruler against skin. Only, for a fifteen-year-old high school girl, any punishment from the principal would certainly not involve a beating with a strap. When I saw the principal from the hallway, the sounds of their shoes against the wood seemed to get louder and louder, and I closed my eyes to hold back the tears.

The room is small, without a window and lit with fluorescent bulbs. I don't remember what I see. A small body wrapped in plastic. It could be Timothy. It could be someone else's son. I

25

close my eyes to hold back the tears, and I nod yes, anxious for a less quiet place. When his body is made to look like his, I will look and see.

Evening comes quick. By the time I leave the funeral director's office, the sun is like an orange half-circle in the sky. It looks like a picture Timothy would have colored. Too much orange, and the color falling outside the lines to fill all the space on the page.

Orange Valley market is nearly closed. Market women are everywhere, shouting prices per pound and grabbing at the late-evening shoppers to get them to buy the last remaining items. The first woman to grab my arm holds up fat ginger, dirt filling the crevices. She looks at me with hope, and I look back with my sad eyes. She lets go of my arm.

"My last piece o' yam. Do, lady, I begging you?"

I turn my sad eyes and open my palms.

Away from the market, the trucks with engines running, the voices from men hoisting boxes and bags into the open trucks, surround me, make me feel less lonely. Away from all the activity, Orange Valley is not so busy. By the time the sounds die away, it is nearly dark. The buses when they get to me are too crowded, filled with higglers and shoppers, unsold goods and purchased goods. I choose to walk instead.

The moon comes up slowly, opposite of where the sun went down. It, too, blazes, and it looks as if the sky is on fire. I remember another night like this, the summer I met Timothy's father. Grams and I were shelling peas. I looked up and saw the orange ball. I touched Grams's arm, pointed to the sky, incapable of saying the simple words, "Look there."

"Come quick," she said. And we hurried inside to watch the flaming moon from a distance. We didn't go back outside that night.

Although I am alone, I hear the women's voices still.

*"An' all the talk people talking 'bout abortion is a sin. Then this no a greater sin than abortion. Standing up there an' watching you own pickney drown."*

*"Is true wha' you say. It better she did kill it before it born."*

*"No. I don't believe that at all. Is wickedness whether you kill the chile before it born or after. I wouldn' say any sin greater than the other. I sure the Bible don' say nothin' 'bout no different degrees of heat in hell. We all goin' burn down there whether we think we commit a little sin or a big one."*

*"No, man. One mus' worse than the other. She stan' there and watch the pickney drown like that. This mus' goin' haunt her for de res' a her life."*

*"An he was such a sweet chile too. Suppose you see him at church. Bright-eyed, don' miss nothin' that go on roun' him. Bright too. Always singing the hymns even though he was so young. . . ."*

But there are other voices I imagine. *There are no women here. Only ladies.*

I carry those words with me still, hold them as I once held the jippi jappa straw hat that accompanied our navy blue tunics and white blouses. That was another life. Westwood High. My one escape from Standfast. Among crowds of girls competing for trophies—speech, debating, Spanish festival, dance—the jippi jappa wearers stood out. In Kingston, Montego Bay, Mandeville, St. Ann's Bay—anywhere—the jippi jappa girls were always ladies with decorum. Black, polished shoes. Perfectly folded socks. Blue cloth badge, with yellow embroidery, always neatly attached. No corners curling inward because a lazy girl forgot to sew on a missing press stud. Collars white. Stray hairs brushed down and back, the imprint of the jippi jappa invisible.

*Even out of uniform, you're representing the school. So as you go home for the summer break, make sure to behave appropriately.*

Andrea, my best friend from school, said once that Principal Pinnock stopped her because she stood outside her father's car with a bottled drink. "No eating or drinking on the street." She imitated perfectly Mrs. Pinnock's quavering voice, the pointed finger.

"Not even candy?" Andrea asked, bold because she was in her father's presence, and out of uniform.

"No eating on the street."

Her father only shook the principal's hand, ready for business.

What would the old girls think if they saw me now? The girl who got the deportment prize two years straight. Black shoes always shiny despite the dust and rain. Rubbed with hibiscus petals if there was no polish around. Buffed with a soft cloth and brush. Pleated skirt for PE always pressed. Evening white dresses and socks as perfect as newly picked cotton. Back straight. Legs crossed. No slouch. Hair parted straight. Braids neat. Then, a perfect girl.

I know what Standfast is saying. What would the others in that so-distant world say of the girl-being-groomed-to-be-a-lady now incapable of stopping a group of children throwing stones, and surrounded by a cackle of loud and raucous women? The same girl who got the prize for elocution in eighth grade, who took home her prize—*Roget's Thesaurus*—and wrapped it in brown paper before she opened it for summer use? The girl who spoke near-perfect English. Good diction. A surprisingly eloquent girl, some teachers said.

There are no ladies here in Standfast; only women.

*But look now! What a waste.* That is what they would say.

Grams is by the roadside, standing outside the croton hedge, when I get there. She has the kerosene lamp at her foot, the dog Pinky lying at her feet.

"What take you so long?"

"Couldn't get no bus, Grams."

"Oh."

She strains to look at my face as if something should be there. We've been together a long time, Grams and I. My mother is one of the few women in Standfast who left home. I don't remember her much, but I remember her back when I waved good-bye. She married a man in New York whom Grams and I don't know. But I'll meet him soon. Things have gotten better for my mother, and I'll be leaving Grams to enter a whole new world.

Almost as soon as we are inside, Pinky barks. A single bark. She is a useless dog.

"Hello," Pam calls from the verandah.

29

Grams shuffles back outside with the kerosene lamp. Yesterday, Pam came by with the clothes I had been washing Thursday when Timothy drowned. Now she has more dry clothes folded stiff in a basin that she carried on her head.

Grams fingers the pieces of cloth. "No. These must be for somebody else."

Pam lingers, shifting her feet in the dirt outside the house, sometimes sliding her foot into the patches of grass.

"We tried, you know, ma'am," she says to Grams. "But nothin' you can do when things a'ready gone too far. The water was in there a'ready, done fill up his lungs before we could do nothin' to save him."

She mostly ignores me, her eyes following her feet and shifting from side to side when she looks at me. She doesn't look me in the eye directly, and I begin to imagine her as one of the women from the river, talking about the way I watched my child drown without doing anything to help him. I am surprised she wasn't with the other women today.

Grams nods her head. She keeps standing, not wanting to sit down and make Pam stay longer. But Pam doesn't go, even after I thank her three times for bringing our clothes back. I know she wants to say something else, probably tell Grams, when I have gone off far enough so I can't hear, that I was responsible for Timothy's drowning.

Pam backs away when Grams blows out the lamp. Pinky barks once again, just lifting her head and not bothering to move at all.

Pam's light is flickering still. I can see it though she is a way off. The voices linger too; always with me.

*"How you mean she didn't see him?"*

*"Tha's what she say. She say she had her back turn to the boy, and she never see him walk in the water."*

*"Then you would leave you' baby like that near water an' no look on him?"*

*"He was sleepin' when she left him there. Sure you don' watch your children every minute."*

*"No. Not every minute. But I wouldn't watch them walk into water like that an' not do nothin' to save them."*

"Kelithe, don't min' what them same bad-minded people here saying at all," Grams says. She returns to the verandah without the lamp. We stand together in the dark. "I hear all of what them saying. All the talk goin' 'round. I know you love that boy and you wouldn't mek him drown."

"Yes, Grams."

"You have business to look 'bout, don't make them stop you. You is a strong girl." Grams repeats things, pats me on my back. And her words remind me of the things she said when my mother left years ago. "Soon," she said. Only, her soon and my mother's soon didn't seem to have an end.

Grams doesn't go into town as often as she used to. But she gets around, hears things. Maisey from next door comes often, telling her everybody's business. She must have told her about the crowd at the funeral parlor.

Around us the crickets are singing, chirping, sounding the way I imagine the stars up above would sound if they were closer, if they could sing. Mosquitoes fly in low, buzz around our ears, and every now and then one of us claps her hands together, hoping one of the mosquitoes is squashed between our palms.

"Yes, A catch you. That will teach you," Grams usually says—a postmortem for the dead mosquito—before wiping her own blood and probably mine from the palms of her hands.

"You think 'bout what you goin' do yet?"

"What you talking 'bout, Grams?"

"What you think? Going back wid you' mother after the funeral. Is Sunday she coming, you know."

"Only a little. You know you can' stay by yourself, Grams. We have to figure that out first."

"I might be old, but I not cripple yet. I can take care o' myself. Long time I on this earth. Time for you to look 'bout you' own self now. Look 'bout you' own business. Not every-thing in life come easy, and sometimes when it come you just have to take it and go on with it."

Look 'bout my own business. But the voices drown out the thoughts of my future.

*"I tell you, they should hol' her under the water and mek she feel wha' it feel like to drown like that."*

*"No punishment can ever be sweeter than a taste o' her own medicine."*

*"And it shouldn't be just a one-time thing. Tek her to the river every week and hol' her head under the water till she start to choke. Just keep on repeating it. That way she'll never forget what the wrong she do. She won't have time to forget 'cause by the time she get it out of her mind is time for the next dose of the medicine."*

*"All them criminals they have down here lock up in jail doing nothin' but just eatin' food and gettin' fat . . . that's what they should do with them too. Give them a dose of their own medicine. Kill them slowly, as the song say."*

*"I tell you, you know, some people must n' have children at all."*

Their talk brings my baby back to life. And I worry that the women who pulled my son's body out of the water will come up behind me some day and accidentally push me into the river. I don't go there to Rio Minho anymore.

# Stirrings

～

*T*he young women, who could only dream of escaping Standfast to work as maids at the hotels on the north coast or with middle-class families, left the funeral home the way they had come. Like one body. They moved slowly, despite the heat. And except for kerchiefs moving across their brows, a folded sheet of newspaper held up by one woman like a visor, the bodies crisscrossing the road for the areas shaded by trees, anyone looking on would think the women didn't feel the heat of the sun or perhaps weren't even certain where they were. Minibuses, cars, vans, trucks loaded with goats, cows, and men, sped by the women, who seemed not to notice the vehicles swerving suddenly toward the center of the road and away from the narrow paths on the roadside that had been defined by the beating of thousands of feet. It didn't matter to the women that they were walking on the busy main road from Orange Valley and not the infrequently used dirt roads that ran through Standfast. A serious accident could have occurred when the vehicles swerved suddenly, and each would have said the same: "I never see or hear anything."

No one spoke, but each woman thought the same thought: It can't end so. All for what? So she can go a foreign?

The women considered the incident at the funeral home another defeat. Not a defeat of them as individuals, but another defeat of their town. A story like the one the older people told about Standfast's failed potential, the one the younger people now regarded as a folktale. Twice Standfast had been let down, and the incidents surrounding the two-day-old tragedy were shaping up to be a third snubbing. The police showed no interest in Standfast's tragedy, in the drowning that looked like an accident but which they were certain amounted to more than that. This outsider chased them off his property but would have welcomed them as individuals, softened his attitude, had he been getting their money.

No, the women thought, it can't end like this.

The women remembered what not many people in Standfast now remember about how the town got its name. Dim memories from slate-and-chalk school days suggest long battles fought against Spanish and British soldiers, age-old blood turned over and over in the dirt by a fork's sharp prongs, forgotten bones in unfarmed hills. But there had been no fighting at all. The local militia, which had been told to prepare for war, to stand fast for a battle, stood fast. Women and children were left to fend for themselves, to plant the fields, see to the cattle, goats, pigs, make certain the mother goats didn't brush aside their still-nursing kids and let them weaken, starve, and die.

But the property owners in the free village came to an understanding before all-out war began. Without knowing of the deal, the militia stood fast, still prepared to fight.

Somebody may have changed the town's name as a joke, or the name may have been meant to honor those men cheated of their chance to prove themselves. The chosen battlefield has never been weeded and planted, nor appropriated by someone wanting to set up a shop. Whatever the reason behind the name change, and even though many people had forgotten the origin of the town's name, Standfast had stood fast all these years, nestled between two mountains. The abundant rains drawn by the green hills fed its river sometimes to overflowing, watering and washing crops away and making the dry and dusty roads look like muddy shortcuts. Despite the presence of the river and the abundance of water, Standfast hadn't shifted shape. Its houses were built in the rich land close to the river and some at the base of the hills, looking as if they were growing out of the hills, rooted like trees leaning slightly from the face of a hill because of the push of earth from up above. The river, Rio Minho, was its center.

They were women of the river. Like their mothers and mothers' mothers, the women were raised on stories of rivers: the legend of the golden table buried at the river's bottom; Nora and the ackees; the River Mumma and the golden comb. When the sun shines from a certain angle, Rio Minho glistens like gold. It rises and falls like the moon, sometimes round and full, golden in the daylight, silver at night. Each of these women has seen the glistening, has been beckoned by the potential for riches, haunted always by the desire to retrieve the buried treasure. And for good reason. Rio Minho has buried treasure they have each lifted and held. It is the story of that elusive treasure, Standfast's second slighting, that their parents and grandparents have shaped as most important in the definition of their lives. They had been bred to accept defeat as Standfast's lot.

When the women got to Rio Minho, they watched the water push and pull, tearing at the river's banks. They imagined how the force of the water could have pulled at weak three-year-old legs. But their conclusion was still the same: the fault lay with the mother, who was blinded by her desire to leave Standfast, who, as they had been told, would not have been able to leave without finding a place for the boy to stay.

In some places the river meandered, lazy, baring the naked stones and fine gravel on its bed. No one spoke. They stood on the bridge and looked with reverence at the gleam from the water, the reflection bouncing toward the trees, and thought how Standfast had degenerated from a town with promise to become a forgotten place. An out-of-the-way place.

No main roads pass through Standfast; they go around it, as if the engineers knew a secret they wanted to keep from anyone using the roads. Even though the residents had built a still-unpaved road that passed straight through the town and meandered by the river, none of the minibuses that went anywhere used it. It wasn't exactly what anyone from most other parts of the country would call a road, more a pass wide enough for a car, and in some places wide enough for two cars to get by without one having to stop to let the other one by, filled with gravel to keep the dust down. Even though the route from Orange Valley to Alexandria would have been shortened by about ten or more miles, nobody—not the bus drivers, nor the residents of Standfast, nor the people from the towns on either side of Standfast—petitioned the government for better roads to secure traffic through the town. So it remained an out-of-the-way place, and anyone wanting to leave the town walked to either of the two places where the buses stopped to catch a ride to some other place. Not bus stops, just two places where bus drivers stopped to let passengers on and off.

Besides the road the people had built, some government official had long ago ordered the construction of a bridge, now old and rickety.

Happiness had lit through Standfast in the 1930s when the government made its promise and the bridge was built. Preachers praised the bridge's beauty, the engineers' genius, the men who lifted the heavy steel and wood and worked the cranes. Preachers promised God that Standfast would not be altered by greed. Revenue was slated for a nearby school. The town rejoiced. Plans were made for new buildings. Men put in applications for jobs working the equipment that would lift the sand and stone. The men turned the farms over to the women and went to help build the bridge, without pay. They would be paid later. The foundation was necessary first.

The women farmed. The children reaped. People in Standfast seemed to walk on air. Rio Minho had a purpose. When the bridge was done, there was a celebration. Flags were hoisted and raised, whole hogs roasted, ram goats butchered and curried, neck bones boiled in soups. Everybody danced and prayed. Standfast was rededicated to the ancestors who had stood fast and in whose honor the town was named.

A premature celebration: the bridge exceeded the budget,

and there was no money for roads. The government workers departed. Official government vehicles left. The bridge was all that remained of the promise.

The flags that had been raised were buried or burned. And in 1962, when the country celebrated its independent government, Standfast didn't blink. The older folks remembered the bridge, the broken promise. Those too young to remember took their cues from the ones who had been there. The town pulled the memory over its head and went back to being a forgotten place. And later, when private developers came to look over the bridge and Rio Minho and rethink the abandoned project, they were neither ignored nor accommodated by the town. If any questions were asked, answers were given. Just enough. No elaboration. If directions were needed, the visitors were escorted to the bridge, but the visitors made their way out alone.

The bridge, suspended between dirt roads, was a constant reminder of Standfast and Rio Minho's potential, a forgotten promise Standfast could never forget.

The story was the basis of the elder residents' response to everything. The elder people replaced the gravel and sand in the roads when the rains or the river washed most of it away. They didn't demand attention from government representatives or sit around waiting for the government to send public works people to come by and build the road or pave it with asphalt. They didn't wait for the members of Parliament who didn't bother stopping in Standfast to secure votes at election time. Those same people went into larger towns to buy the things that deliverymen were not willing to risk their trucks to deliver. Those people carried water from the river to their homes to make up for the lack of running water and didn't complain to any unknown member of Parliament about what they lacked. They lit candles and kerosene lamps at night, shooed tiny bats away from the flickering flames, and shared kerosene or coal when one family was without. No one checked in with the Rural Electrification Program to determine how far down on the list Standfast appeared and how much time would pass before electricity came to Standfast.

The failure of the Rio Minho project, the isolation of the town, were the two things that shaped the way Standfast's elders viewed the town in relationship to the remainder of the island. And this knowledge they fed the young as if Standfast were trapped in an endless maze, dizzied and forever defeated.

But these young women of the river, even further removed from Standfast's failed attempt at glory, wanted to view the legend of Rio Minho's failed potential as a folktale. They had dreams and expectations that mirrored the dreams of their warrior ancestors. They were tired of sitting back and watching Standfast wait.

These young women watched the river and secretly gloated because once again something tragic had happened to the girl who had gone off to boarding school and whose mother regularly sent barrels from America. The first tragic thing had been Kelithe's early pregnancy. The baby brought Kelithe back to their level. They no longer viewed her as the girl who had passed the Common Entrance Exam, gone to high school, and come back talking and acting differently, but the girl who had come back from a boarding school six months pregnant, a girl like themselves who sat back and waited for something good to come. They wanted the third tragic thing involving Kelithe to be justice for the drowned child, because no woman, no mother, had a right to do what they said Kelithe had done. The desire to leave, they could forgive. But a mother forgetting her duty to her child—that they could not forgive.

The women convinced themselves that their desire to see justice served had nothing to do with the fact that Kelithe still could escape Standfast and relocate to America, a feat they still didn't have the means to accomplish. Had the situation concerned any other woman, they told themselves, they would still have wanted a police investigation. Without discussing the day, they separated for their homes to prepare the evening meals.

The tragedy took over their lives as nothing ever had. Their passion made them forget things: outdoor fires fanned and stoked to the appropriate, slow burn, but forgotten and left to peter out completely; thyme clippings put in the sun to dry, forgotten and soaked by the fleeting afternoon rain; fresh fish being scaled, forgotten when Pam went to retrieve a lime, and ultimately eaten by hungry dogs; dried corn for the chickens sprinkled in Claudine's hog pen instead of in the chicken coop. Miriam forgot to set basins of water in the sun so the child with cold on his chest and a lingering cough could have warm water for his evening bath. And the afternoon rain increased the chill already in the water.

Afternoon stretched into evening. And not one of the women could count the things they accomplished for the afternoon.

41

Pam headed toward the Marshall's shop to buy codfish to replace the fresh fish she lost to the hungry dogs. She wanted to have something in the pot before her husband came back from the fields with the empty lunch containers and his eyes trained toward the stove.

Claudine told her children she needed to clear her mind, and after chasing them out of the house so she could have some peace and quiet, she left and headed to the Marshall's shop for a small bottle of Red Label wine to ease her troubled mind.

Olive went to get the baked beans she should have picked up at the market earlier in the day when she had joined the band of women who decided to follow Kelithe to the funeral parlor. Baked beans mixed with corned beef, served with flour dumplings, was her children's favorite, and something she didn't mind preparing because she didn't have to bend over the stove too long.

Miriam went to buy bay rum to rub down her son's body and keep away the fever that would surely come if she let the already sick boy bathe in cold water.

One by one the women left their houses and headed to the town center, as if pulled by a common string, dazed, drawn by their shared passion to see some form of justice done. They stood under the poinciana tree outside the Marshall's shop, protected from the evening sun by an arc of green leaves. The flaming flowers had withered, and all the long green seedpods had turned black and fallen to the ground, mingling with over-ripe mangoes from a nearby tree.

"It can't end so," they grumbled, shook their heads, and turned their sad eyes toward the damp ground.

Pam lifted her eyes first and said she would make her own pilgrimage to the police station in Orange Valley, describe detail by detail what happened Thursday at Rio Minho. She punctuated her words by slapping one of the dried pods against her left palm. The seeds inside rattled.

"No," the chorus responded.

"We tried that a'ready, and see, nothin' happen yet." When Lucille spoke, she slapped the back of her right hand against her open left palm for emphasis. Her eyes widened, and she looked at each face. "Whatever we do, it has to be done here. By Standfast. Not the police."

The nine women stood in their close group, mindful of nothing but their desire to mete out punishment. Men returning from the fields they had worked for the day passed the group of women. The men walked slowly behind donkeys with hampers full of the day's produce. The men shouted their greetings, turned their heads slowly so as not to upset the banana bunches balanced on mats of dried banana leaves and placed on their heads. The women nodded in return, too caught up to put out more effort.

Two children ran by, pushing an old tire with a stick. And as each woman turned to look at the laughing children chasing the tire, she remembered the smell of burning rubber from demonstrations and strikes in Orange Valley two years earlier when the government had refused to vote in favor of raises for public servants. All eyes moved from face to face. But no one spoke.

They moved again as if still linked by that common string. They combed their yards for unused pieces of board, old paint cans, dried tree branches, disused farming tools, worn car tires, their children's broken pushcarts, rusting oil drums, empty barrels, termite-eaten furniture, hamper baskets and market baskets that had lost their bottoms. They didn't have a

43

lot to choose from, but the refuse brought to the central point near the poinciana tree and not far from the Basics School mounted.

Olive, with the help of her husband, Edson, dismantled the pen where they had kept their last hog. Edson gladly knocked the structure down and carried the pieces of board because he had vowed never again to raise pigs. The smell, he said, was the most unbearable thing. Olive, too, carried some of the board and the makeshift gate, constructed from zinc and wood.

Others gathered dried leaves from banana plants, corn husks, dried pea plants from which the pods had been pulled, branches from breadfruit trees. The women gathered their children to help. Little legs wobbled, moved quickly under the wide load that filled the arms.

When they exhausted the refuse around their yards, the women turned to their houses for broken things that simply took up space—the sofas that sat low on the floor because termites had eaten away the wooden legs; broom handles; a radio that no longer worked; the rubber bottoms of well-worn sneakers; leather shoes stained with dirt.

When Olive was done gathering things in her yard, she grabbed other women, and the small group headed in the weak evening light toward the fields the men had worked during the day. They walked among the freshly dug yam hills, looking for old dried vines, cane and corn stalks cut and thrown aside, cabbage leaves that would otherwise have been gathered for rabbits, leaves cut from the tops of cane stalks, as well as the cane peel. They took anything that could be burned.

The women, accustomed to building slow fires on coal stoves, sprinkled a few drops of kerosene on the heap of garbage, and started a fire that they wanted to grow slowly and not peter out. Other than Lisette saying, "One this way, and one on the other side," the women worked in silence, prodding the things they had brought, pushing them closer to the center of the fire, and beating down the flames to make certain the fire didn't flare too high.

The fire caught and spread slowly, concentrated in the center. When the fire bloomed, the mixture of odors was the one thing that would have made the women reconsider their actions. Instead, they covered their noses, stepped back, and recalled other more pungent odors like the smell of a pit latrine or pigpen where lime had not been placed to neutralize the odor.

They weren't absolutely certain why they were blocking a road that was rarely used by motor vehicles, but that was the way, they knew, other Jamaican towns voiced displeasure, made their grievances heard.

# The Promise

*I* didn't always love him. At first, no. That I'm guilty of.

"Nobody can love him as much as you," Grams said.

Grams folded my arms around him, kept her hands—which felt as if she had been rubbing pimento seeds on the sieve—around me. In those early days she made sure I kept him in my arms. Constantly. Whenever I put him down, left him for too long lying alone on the bed, she cut her eyes at me and muttered under her breath. When he was about a week old, she wrapped him in sheets and covered his head with one of the knitted caps my mother had sent.

"Come with me down to Miss Maisey." She pushed shoes on my feet, helped me from the bed, and prodded me from behind.

On the way down the hill, she didn't speak. It was as if I

wasn't there. She didn't take the shortcut through the cocoa fields, the place we call Cocoa Walk, but walked the long way on the road. We took our time getting there, I limping, she walking as if she weren't holding a one-week-old baby. She didn't knock on the door when we came upon the house, but walked around back to where Miss Maisey kept her goats at night. There was a kid bawling, trying to stand on wobbly feet. Its mother lay down and butted the kid away when it came near her.

"Somebody touch the kid tail, and now the mother don't want him," Grams said. "Maisey have to mix milk powder and feed it from a baby nipple bottle just to keep it alive."

She turned away, and we went back toward home without stopping at Maisey's door.

"You were almost never born." She threw the words back at me.

This time we went through Cocoa Walk. New leaves from vines and bushes were forcing their way into the broken-down path, tickling my bare legs. I worried about ticks and frogs.

"She was 'bout three months along, and she nearly kill you."

I hadn't known this before. The thought of almost not being born made me shudder. The devil walking on what could have been a baby girl's grave. I thought then and still think now of the things I came close to never knowing: the sun rising, going down at night; the sweetness of cane juice, naseberries, overripe otaheite apples; the sticky sweet of a ripe mango. I came close to never knowing the feeling of lying on water, floating with the river downstream. Floating on and on with the current to the sea where the river goes. My mother came close to never allowing me to know the feel of river water rush-

47

ing along, slapping against my feet, lifting my body with each rise and fall of gentle waves.

I almost never came to know the feel of soft sand squishing between my toes, slipping under my feet. The tickling feel of an ant crawling over my leg. The soft touch of my baby's fingers. Experiences Timothy will never have.

"Two times you nearly die in her womb," Grams said then. "Two. When her father fin' out, he whip her with a stick because she did what he never expect any of his own children to do. Chase you' father off and beat his daughter with a stick. I pull him off her. Save you the first time. Save you the second time when she try to kill you herself."

She didn't describe what my mother attempted to do. I didn't ask. The thought of the imaginary grave . . . I wouldn't even have had a grave.

"You live," Grams said. "Came out fighting and bawling like something inside there was choking you. Nothing like the other children I deliver."

Some of those other children she delivered came feetfirst and had to be turned around inside their mothers. She told me about those babies, some that the mothers wouldn't take, wouldn't love, and those who were smothered by their mothers' love the minute they were born. I wish she had told me what it was like for me, whether my mother had smothered me with her love, or whether Grams was the one who had welcomed me, warmed me with her body heat.

When we got back to the house, she laid Timothy on the bed. "Whatever you thinking, you can't punish him for your own mistake. That I tell your mother one time, and the same I telling you now."

I tried to say, "Yes, ma'am," tell her I was only tired, but she said, "No, hush. He won't love nobody else the way he love you. Think 'bout the way you love your mother. When she lef', you bawl eye water every day."

I never forget.

I think of my mother's leaving when I think of my son. Her soon-soon promise.

"Not right now," she said when I pulled on her skirt and begged her to take me. "Can't take you now. Just a little while till I settle down and things get good.

"Maybe in a year or two I'll send for you."

I was five then, and a year or two didn't mean much. After five came six and after six came seven. That's all. Not 730 days or twenty-four months till she came again, before I would be with her in that place I didn't know.

"Soon, soon," she said.

Grams said the same when I asked. "Soon. Soon she'll come back and get you."

She forgot to kiss me good-bye. For a long time all I remembered of my mother was her forgotten good-bye kiss. Her arms around my grandmother. Her lips on Grams's cheek, then mouth. Her body pressed close to Grams. Her stiff, starched dress pressing into my unstarched dress. A hug. The falling away of the stiff dress. The smoothing of the stiff dress, a brush down as if she were brushing me away from her.

A stiff dress handing passport and papers to a woman sitting by the door. A glass painted blue. The dress behind the blue glass. Fingers waving good-bye. A soon-soon promise.

That's the way I remember the day she left and forgot to kiss me good-bye. Left me in Standfast with a bottomless promise so I could hear her voice every few months, when Grams and I would go to the phone booth and stand in line behind everyone else who had someone to call.

Her voice changed after she left, crackling sometimes because of the static on the line. At other times she just sounded foreign, like a different person, using words I'd never heard, calling things by names I didn't know, speaking more like an American than a Jamaican.

It hurts to go back that far. But when I think about Timothy, I think too about my mother's leaving.

I didn't want to leave him behind. Ever. I didn't want him to think of his mother as always going away, to remember me mostly by the shape of my retreating back and the way I waved my fingers good-bye.

# Standfast

~

There was no welcoming sign to Standfast. There had been none when Sonya left, and now she wasn't surprised that there was nothing, except for cows and goats tethered by the side of the road, that signaled a whole town lay within. At both roads to the town were huge rocks on which people sat when they waited for the bus, and the papers and candy wrappers they dropped were sometimes the only clues that someone had been by.

She had observed the island, hoping for some small change in Standfast, perhaps the long-promised school. She didn't see a new building that looked like a school. Back when she was still small, she had heard word that the government was planning to build a new secondary school nearby, at least one that was closer than the one in Orange Valley. But when her time came, she joined the others on the early-morning walk to the bus stop and on the minibuses to the secondary school in Orange Valley; the talk of the school never amounted to more than just talk.

The rest of the country had changed, so why not Standfast? There were new buildings in every town through which she drove, constructed without a formal town plan. Some of the buildings jutted out into the street, while others were set back from the road with clearly marked parking spaces and cloth awnings advertising their purpose, towering new two- and three-story buildings with burglar bars across the windows and doors, next to old Spanish-style buildings. But it was the number of new and half-built houses—with curtains hanging in the windows of the lower painted portions of the house and naked concrete and steel protruding from the upper portions—that surprised her most. She wondered if the houses leaked and how safe the residents felt living in a house with only a ceiling instead of a sturdy roof. She saw as many completely built houses as she saw half-built ones, some large, some small, most with burglar bars covering their windows.

There were also the numerous new resorts built conveniently close to the sea. Sand Castles Resorts. Sea Castles Resorts. White Gothic-style castles inches from the sea. Ocean Breeze Resorts. Oceana. Island Sun. Pastel-colored or white buildings shaded by bougainvillea vines, palm, hibiscus trees. After a while she no longer noticed their names, just saw the pink-and-white structures, inviting, beautiful, opulent. She imagined the sound of the waves crashing against rocks, the sand, at night, the salt-laden air blowing through the rooms. Unhappy people happy to be working, to be earning. Perhaps happy to have escaped a place like Standfast, to borrow comfort and softness for brief moments of the day.

"No planning," she had muttered on her way out of Montego Bay. "No planning at all. Everybody in a hurry but can't sit back to plan anything good."

But she couldn't say the same for Standfast. There was no hurry in the pace of this place, almost no movement at all.

Sonya wasn't surprised that the first thing she noticed when she got there was the old man everybody called Hush Puppies because he'd gone away on farm work for three years and brought back three pairs of Hush Puppies each for his wife and three children. He was lounging by the bar, his back against a wooden column, a brown Red Stripe beer bottle in one hand and a homemade cane in the other. She remembered him because Hush Puppies was the person she thought of the one time she considered packing up and coming back home to Jamaica. She recalled the emptiness in his eyes, one hand clutching a beer bottle and the other turned up as if he were waiting for something to fill the empty space. It was that emptiness and her own memory of always wanting more that made her stay in New York despite the winters and the thought that she would have one daughter who she never really knew and one she knew too well.

Standfast boasted none of the half-finished houses, none of the unplanned commercial buildings, she had seen elsewhere across the island. The road still hadn't been paved. There were no light poles, so she knew electricity hadn't yet come to the town, that the people in Kingston who ran the government's Rural Electrification Program hadn't reached that section of the country.

53

She had turned the air conditioner on as soon as she got into the car at the airport, so she didn't smell smoke or the stench of burning rubber and didn't suspect that there indeed had been a change until she came upon the fire blazing in the middle of the road. It was the overturned car, partially burned, that made her realize it was a roadblock and not just somebody burning garbage in the wrong place. There were a few people standing around, most of them children. But she thought there should have been a lot more people, tending the fire and keeping it ablaze and holding up signs so she knew what the protest was all about. Nobody looked her way. The children ran circles around the fire, a few pushing green wheels made from garden hose and others just jumping around and laughing.

Sonya didn't roll the window down until the man she had seen walking toward the car was right upon it.

"Afternoon, ma'am. De roadblock, you know, ma'am. Can' pass this way."

"This the only roadblock?"

"No. One or two more. But you can go all the way aroun' and come back up de other way if that will get you where you wan' go."

"Thanks." She nodded and put the car in reverse.

She told herself she hadn't liked the way he peered into the car, shifted his head to look at the boxes on the backseat as if confirming that she was a visitor, a foreigner.

A few roadblocks on the single road through Standfast, and she had to turn back and go nearly fifteen miles out of her way to come up to the town the other way. In a town that had very little traffic or none at all, who would see the protest, or care that the residents of this out-of-the-way town had grievances they wanted heard? And she wasn't even certain if the one or two other roadblocks the man had mentioned were before or after the turnoff to her mother's house.

Nothing on the drive from the airport had prepared Sonya for this small, not-so-successful demonstration in Standfast; there had been no reports on the radio of disturbances in any part of the country, unless she had missed the news on those occasions that the radio faded out when she drove under trees or in the valley regions. All the roads had been clear and free except for some recklessly driven minibuses and tourists who swerved unnecessarily because they weren't certain if they were driving on the left side of the road.

And even if there had been some government plan or perceived injustice that riled people across the country, she was certain Standfast wouldn't be a part of the demonstration. She didn't remember any political controversy that had incited the town, that had set Standfast on edge, that had made the residents organize or seek a political voice. Standfast had made do.

Sonya recalled no celebrations in 1962 when the British had granted independence. No trips planned to the National Stadium to witness for themselves the August 5 midnight lowering of the Union Jack, the symbolic denouncement of 307 years of British rule. No trips to see the black, green, and gold Jamaican flag hoisted in its place. No black, green, and gold flags waved in the air. No drums. No release of pent-up screams. No dances or parades. Nothing, even though events of the past should have dictated that Standfast, so named because it had stood fast in a long-ago war against the enemy, rejoice that the freedom it had been ready to fight for so long ago had finally come.

The politics of the late 1970s and early 1980s that polarized Kingston—the socialists against the laborites—didn't touch Standfast. Nobody voted. The officials forgot to designate a polling station, and no one in Standfast pursued the oversight. The town elders didn't discuss the merits of the socialists, the potential benefits of an alliance with Cuba, or consider what would be lost if Michael Manley succeeded in building a socialist nation. Cuba and its cane fields would be the promised land. Nobody debated how much the country would sacrifice if it did not elect Edward Seaga and align with the United States, how many family members would possibly be cut off, denied reentry into their homeland. No politicians came to persuade eligible voters to cast their ballots for one party or the other.

Sonya came to the other end and nearly missed the road for the bushes that obscured it, making it seem like a shortcut for people to walk through rather than a road built for traffic. Nearly missing the road, added to the annoyance of having to drive about fifteen miles out of her way, stirred up the aggravation that should have come on once she approached the roadblock and didn't know the reason she had to go out of her way. Her annoyance was more pronounced because she disliked herself a little for showing so much interest in a place she had been so eager to leave. She needed to compare her progress, to think about where she would have been had she stayed in the slow-moving Standfast.

The road on this end of the town was worse than the other end, worse than she remembered it being. She wondered if the river had overflowed one time too many and washed away the sand and stones that had been put there to keep the dust down. Sonya thought, too, of the many times the men went into the river and scraped the bed for sand and stones to fill the spots in the road where the heavy rains had washed the stones away. But they seemed to have forgotten this end of the road. The road on the other side had been much smoother; she hadn't heard the things in the back of the car rolling around each time she drove over a pothole or swerved to avoid a big hole in the road.

There was a small roadblock on this end—not a fire, just things stacked up in the street waiting for the matches and kerosene to set it ablaze. Sonya got out of the car this time and walked toward a little shop not far from the roadblock.

"Afternoon, sir. Any way I can get through?"

The old man behind the counter looked at her as if he recognized the face behind the sunglasses. He nodded and went toward the back of the shop, to what she knew was where he and his family lived.

"Jimmy, Jimmy." Sonya listened to his hoarse voice and tried to put a name to his face. "Come let this foreigner through."

When the old man returned, he lifted his head as if wanting his chin to point the way. "He goin' let you through."

"Thanks." Sonya thought her thanks was as weak as quickly brewed tea, mostly because she couldn't remember the man's name to thank him properly or ask about the health of his family. When she walked out of the store, she wondered, too, if she should have bought something or given him money for his trouble. But she knew that giving him money outright would be the biggest insult.

The boy Jimmy was pushing some of the tree branches to the side of the road. It wouldn't take long to push the branches away or clear enough room for the car to pass. Nobody in Standfast had that much to throw away or burn. It was mostly branches, old paint cans, well-worn tires, and something looking like the rusted door of a car.

She stood on the shop steps, feeling the heat through the zinc roof and looking out at the unmanned roadblocks and the narrowing of the road at the end of the town through which she'd just passed. It was the quiet that bothered her most, a quiet like that of a jungle animal waiting to pounce, a vicious dog waiting at his master's gate for any unknown person to plant his feet on his master's ground, a teacher waiting to catch a child cheating off his neighbor's test paper. Nobody seemed to be around and about. Not that Standfast was anything close to a bustling town, but in her younger days there had always been somebody looking to sell something or exchange one thing for another, or more children playing in the streets. And while there had been children running around at the first roadblock that she had come across, the adults were strangely missing. Except for the one man who came to tell her what she already knew: that the road was blocked. And even here at the other end, Jimmy and his father, who sat in the near-empty shop, seemed to be the only ones manning this roadblock, which needed kerosene, a match light, and a lot more material to get a real fire going. Besides people, Sonya thought something else was missing: the charged electricity of a protest, of people demanding and expecting change. Maybe the change in Standfast lay with one group ready to fight, unlike the people of her youth.

Even the river seemed quiet. She didn't hear the strong rush of water she had imagined, which made her think it hadn't been raining very much at all. The river now must not be very full, definitely not close to overflowing. She didn't hear any of the women who gathered there at all times of day to wash—no laughter or song, even though she had turned the window down and listened for some long-ago sounds. She didn't hear the children's laughter, or the sounds of cooking, or see men digging in the fields. No cows lowing, or goats. If it hadn't been for the three men she had seen, the children playing around the fire on the other side, the fire itself, she would have thought Standfast was deserted.

The quiet wasn't peaceful. It was bothersome.

The roadblocks bothered Sonya, too. Because the roadblocks were out of character. Because she thought the roadblocks divided the town between those who would fight and those who wouldn't. Because the roadblocks seemed like a waste with no outsiders to witness or put out the effort to make the change that a protest should demand.

It was the energy that was missing—the conviction that the protest in Standfast was worth it, would yield some results.

Sonya watched Jimmy push the debris aside. From inside the house she heard voices, hoarse whispers like furniture grating against the floor. A female voice asked about the owner of the car.

"She look like a foreigner," the man said in reply.

"Mus' Grams's daughter, Kelithe mother. You shouldn't let her through. Mek she walk."

"Let she gwan through. She not the cause o' the problem. Is the girl, Kelithe." 59

Sonya didn't alter her stance, but she suspected they were staring at her back, perhaps with a suspicion similar to that of the man who had peered in her car at the first roadblock. She remembered one of those who had called to relate the death of Timothy had said all Standfast was saying Kelithe had stood and watched the baby drown. But Sonya laid that thought aside and raised up her mother's voice: "Kelithe heart broken. Come see 'bout you' chile."

"There space 'nuff now, ma'am," Jimmy said.

Sonya nodded and got back into the car, ready for the hard rocking from driving over stones and avoiding holes. She didn't have far to go into the back of beyond, into the out-of-the-way, forgotten place.

# Escape

~

It's been a long time in coming—my second escape from this out-of-the-way, forgotten place. Standfast.

The one thing that's been holding me back is what brought me back here. The secret flesh, growing inside me, stretching the skin over my stomach. A ball of tissue, my biology books say, growing eyes, ears, hands, fingers, feet. It. The baby.

Waves of stretch marks across my stomach, lighter than the brown of my stomach, a few shades lighter than the dark-chocolate-colored skin on my arms, face, legs. Stretch marks that itch and don't go away. Soaking up the cocoa butter lotion I rub on my secret bulge.

Navel popping out, my blood pumping through the vessels of the flesh growing inside me. Feeding the fetus that forces me to throw up the little I can stomach. Swelling my breasts, my feet, my hands, my nose. My nostrils flaring wider, seeming to cover half my face. My dark skin looking even darker, almost black, and my thick, pink lips looking as if they too have expanded to match my swollen nose. My hair growing thicker and much faster than I have ever known it to grow.

My pregnancy is a biology lesson. The sperm fertilizes the egg, forming a union that's beyond my control now. One cell, dividing and dividing and dividing, and then growing inside me.

Nine months. Twenty-eight weeks. Twenty-nine weeks. Each month more, and more, just a little bit more of the swelling, the stretching. Painless stretching. But inside me the pain, the anxiety, the thoughts of hurting myself or this baby, returning myself to the sweet innocence of virginity, finding the child that my mother sent away to school to learn how to be a lady.

I am a woman, all right. Just not the woman my mother ever thought I would be. All this before it became Timothy. Drawing stares because I'm so young. Still a student, really, and a failure.

At school our guidance counselor would say, "All you who love to laugh are the first ones who're going to lie down." Girls always ready for gossip. We watched and we pointed our fingers outward, never inward, at the girls we thought would be the first to leave school with a melon belly. We pointed at the girls the prefects ferreted out of dark corners, blinding them with the white light of their flashlights, on our annual fair day when town people, our parents, friends, everyone, came together to help raise money for the school and liberate the boarding students from the monotony of boarding life.

Nobody expected the belly woman to be me.

*     *     *

I knew I was pregnant by the blood that was dripping out of me, slowly, drop by drop. It wasn't the usual flow, not the thick red blood that came regularly, knocking me out with its pain, building cramps deep in the bottom of my belly or in my lower back. For four days there were bright red drops, one or two each day. I hoped, I waited, I watched for the few drops to build into a large mass, a continuous stream flowing from my body, telling me everything was okay. I prayed. I waited out the first month, the second, watching my stomach swell and round out beneath my uniform and my white dresses, watching and waiting for my food to come crawling back up from the pit of my stomach.

My secret. My baby. Mine to love. Mine to hate. All mine.

Even when I was sure, I waited. It was too early, too soon. Still time, early enough so nobody would know. I waited. Waited, sitting in classrooms, studying, thinking, adding, subtracting numbers and letters that meant nothing to me, reading Shakespeare, Jean Rhys. Writing essays that had nothing to do with feeding a baby. Marking my pregnancy like it was a biology experiment.

*Embarazada* is the word for "pregnant" in Spanish. Sounds like "embarrassed."

Teenage pregnancy. Still not common at this girl's boarding school. One, maybe two pregnancies each school year among the five hundred or so girls. Ladies. Fashioned after age-old British customs. One of the last holdouts of English colonial values and rules. The straw hats, worn long ago by British colonialists to break the sun's heat, are still part of our uniform.

White dresses in the evenings for the boarders. White slips, white bras, black panties underneath the white-white dresses. Angel suits. Ladies.

Six months, before the whispers among the boarders turn to spoken sentences around the dining table at breakfast, at lunch, at dinner. Six months of loosening the zipper on the side of my tunic, loosening the cotton material that is stretched across my bulging stomach, slipping my hand through the opening to rub the itching stretch marks, calm the baby's kicking.

Six months, knowing I can't go on for much longer without everyone noticing the round, pronounced shape of my stomach, wearing a sweater all day long in this sweltering Jamaican heat. I avoid PE with lies, my own doctor's note.

Six months before Mrs. Pinnock, our principal, believes the whispers she has heard. But not before she has punished the other six girls in my dorm with order marks, permanently written into their school transcripts, for spreading malicious lies. Not before she has made them wash the dishes after supper, sweep up bits of windblown paper around the schoolyard, and forfeit their weekends home. Two weeks of standing under the bell during our fifteen-minute morning break between classes, watching the other students watching them—Andrea, Denise, Karla, Michelle, Claudette, Keisha—and whispering about the imagined reasons for their punishment. Two weeks of punishment for whispering about my swollen stomach that they have seen outlined beneath my thin nightgown, and which they know is hidden during the daylight hours by an oversize sweater.

"What happen? You sick?" Andrea, one of those punished, my best friend, asked early on, a month after I first suspected I was pregnant.

"I tell you all the time I can't stand the smell of the boiled eggs we get for breakfast."

"You going to Nurse McIntosh?"

"No. Wha' you think she going give me? Prob'ly milk of magnesia, and that only going make things worse. Make me throw up some more."

"Well, if you go to the nurse, you can lie down over there. You don't have to go to PE."

"Yeah. Maybe."

"You sure is the egg? You never used to throw up like this before when they used to boil the eggs the same way. You suddenly come back from summer holiday, and you can't stand the smell of boiled eggs anymore!"

"You can't tell me what making me sick. I know is the egg." Andrea is my best friend, yet I can't tell her I suspect that I'm pregnant.

Two girls from two different worlds, drawn together by similar classes, a lab table shared in seventh grade. Four years later, and we are still feeling our way around each other, not sure what will embarrass each other, change our friendship to the soft-shoe steps of early friendship.

She doesn't know much about my hometown, Standfast. She doesn't know my grandmother's house is illuminated every night by kerosene lamps, glass lamps with "Home Sweet Home" written on the fragile shades. Or candles that burn down too quickly. She doesn't know about my mother.

I can't tell her my secret.

It's not that I lie about where I come from. I tell everyone the memories are not pleasant and that I would rather forget the past.

Rumors never die on their own, and especially not at boarding schools, where all lives are intertwined by shared bathrooms, bedrooms, and where all news is limited to what filters in with the day students, or letters from home.

"There's been a lot of rumors going around here," Principal Pinnock says. She peers over her glasses when she speaks. "Is there any truth to what I'm hearing?"

"Rumors about what?"

"Don't get smart with me, young lady! Are you pregnant?"

"Yes, miss."

Even though she has seen my rounded stomach in the nurse's office—my tunic off, the waist-length white cotton blouse buttoned at the top only—she takes me to the doctor before she calls my mother to take me away from the school.

My mother comes. She hides her shame, shuts her face like a window, and holds her head high as she leads me away from Westwood, the place she sent me so I would have more than she had in Standfast. But we don't talk about this, the baby that would be Timothy.

My mother returns to New York, and I, to Grams. Standfast. Stand fast. This time there's no soon-soon promise.

Stretching, stretching, but still not wide enough. Not yet. Pain. Blood on my lips. Squirming. Pain. Sucking on air. Sharp quick breaths to dull the pain.

A little bit more.

Push, the doctor says. Push harder. He doesn't know the pain. It's taking too long.

*"She's not fully dilated yet."*
   *"How's the baby's heart rate?"*
   *"Slowing."*
   *"We have to cut. The baby's not getting enough air."*

Swirling in a cloud of blackness and pain.
It.
The baby. Pulled outside to breathe on its own.
Timothy. Curled locks on top of a wrinkled face. Ears darker than the pale brown face, showing his true color, the shade his complexion will darken to in no time at all. Not a trace of his father's features. Wide nose, flared at the nostrils. Tiny hands and feet, with a lot of power to grasp my fingers, kick before his rush of tears.

Timothy. Fatherless. Born to a sixteen-year-old high school dropout.

He, Timothy, brought me back away from boarding school. My one escape. Back to this forgotten place.

# Carrying News

⁓

At first neither Grams nor the young-girl-turned-woman moved. Grams was pulling weeds from near some flowers, and Kelithe removing damp clothes from a piece of zinc. They both looked up, hands to their brows, sheltering their eyes from a sun that was no longer there, as if their hands over their brows made them see better. Neither of them moved until Sonya stepped from the car and put a blue suitcase on the ground. Sonya thought it was her mother who moved first and who turned to tell Kelithe to go and help.

"Evenin', ma'am."

Sonya wanted a friendlier, warmer welcome from her daughter. A hug, perhaps, or a smile.

"How you doing, dear?" Sonya turned as she asked the question and pulled her daughter into her arms. In the brief moment she held her, Sonya thought of her younger daughter, Kris, and the full hugs she got in the evenings when she came home from work or the hugs she got from the children she watched during the days.

It must be her grief, Sonya thought. But except for Kelithe's first five years, and the few days she spent when she came to take her daughter from boarding school, Sonya didn't have many memories, no strong memories of the child to compare to the adult Kelithe to know whether her daughter kept her emotions bottled up inside or let them seep like air from a small hole in a balloon, or like air from the sudden pop of a balloon, so everyone around would share her joy or pain.

Her mother took her time climbing the little hill. And it wasn't till then that she knew that her mother's "Everything all right" over the phone was a lie. Her mother walked with obvious pain, and very slowly, as if a single small stone could upset her delicate balance.

"Mama." Sonya was at once disturbed by the strength of the hug she gave her mother compared to the weaker one she had given her daughter. "You lookin' well."

"You lookin' good too, girl. The flight was all right?"

"Yes, yes. Everything good."

"Glad you reach safe."

Kelithe passed then with the suitcase Sonya had first taken out, straining from the weight.

"She taking everything all right?"

"As good as you can expect."

The place was pretty much the same as it had been during her childhood, except it appeared smaller, as if the land and house had shrunk.

69

Sonya hadn't been there a good thirty minutes before Miss Maisey shuffled into the yard and settled herself as if she were in her rightful place.

In a town with such limited financial resources, Sonya's rented car with its cushioned seats and near-perfect body advertised itself and her presence. Sonya wanted to convince herself that the comfortable, nearly new car, a rarity in Standfast, was the reason the man at the roadblock had stared so intently into the car, the reason Maisey came so quickly to her mother's house.

"Lord, you come," Maisey said. "Sorry it wasn't under better circumstances. But thank God you reach safe." Drawing up one of the low wooden chairs, lowering her body, and facing Sonya, Maisey reached over and patted Sonya's bare arm with her rough palms.

She called out a greeting to Grams and joked about having a new foreign friend to tell her about the rest of the world. She didn't ask about Kelithe, nor did she call out a greeting to the young girl.

Maisey started out innocently enough with talk of who had arthritis, or heart conditions, high blood pressure, the dry spells and the floods, and how good God was to humble people.

"We's a people that make do. And God always like that. Yes. All these young people hurryin', hurryin' after somethin' and forgettin' God like the humble ones."

As Maisey talked she rubbed her own arthritic hands over her swollen knee, her dry hands against the cloth making a sound like crackling paper. She whispered, "Yes, yes," between her statements, and her head bobbed up and down as she lowered and raised her hand.

"You looking good, Maisey."

"Yes, yes. You lookin' good too. The place 'gree wid you."

Maisey didn't give Sonya much chance to talk. As soon as the old lady ended one story, she launched into another as if the connecting ideas were clearly obvious.

"Rio Minho water good now, you know. Water not too low and not too high. Just right. Not too much rains this way at all. Long time now the river don't flood. Rio Minho . . ."

Every now and again Maisey stopped, swallowed hard, probably checking the parts of the story she could tell the mother of the supposed killer, the grandmother of the dead baby. Sonya listened to the sound Maisey's mouth made when she swallowed and readjusted her dentures. She knew the movements from having seen them in the light.

Sonya twisted with discomfort. She told herself she longed to be moving about the house because she had been sitting so much all day, first in the plane and then the long car ride.

Little by little Maisey inched her way to Kelithe's story, the talk of the women who had been there at the river and of those who hadn't.

"They say the water wasn't strong. Barely moving. Rain not falling this way much now. Nothing on top of the water. No branches. Nothing. Just plain ol' water. All of a sudden he was under the water. An' everybody start to run. He went down one, two, three times. Nobody know, you know. But by the time they reach him . . . Nothing. Three time he go under . . ."

Sonya felt guilty for listening to her longtime friend tell the story of her grandson's death. It's a story she thought should come from Kelithe or her mother, not from a stranger who had long ago loved to gossip. In the few hours she had been there, Sonya hadn't asked Kelithe any questions, nor did she mention the baby to Kelithe or her own mother. "I'm sorry for the loss," she had thought of saying to Kelithe when she first saw her daughter-turned-woman standing there. But the words seemed false, strange, and brought back to mind the simple words, *Kelithe watched,* and the nagging Did she? question that had been plaguing her since the day she heard the sad news. She wanted to find the comfort words that she would have said had it been any other woman's child. But she couldn't, and she wondered, if it had been her secondborn, Kris, what she would have said. She thought of simply asking, "How you holding up?" But that question, too, didn't seem to be right; she expected Kelithe's answer to be simply, "All right."

Sonya listened to Maisey because she remembered her initial questions, because she recalled the roadblock and felt something strange was happening in Standfast.

"Some people say they heard him cry. Some never hear nothing, just see the movement out o' the corner o' them eye. I tell you, is a sad way to go. So young."

Dusk closed in, but Sonya didn't move to get a candle or lamp. She felt better not seeing Maisey's face as she told her tale.

"But they say Kelithe stand there and watch. So they say." She said the last as if distancing herself from the accusation. "I wasn't there, but so they say."

"What Standfast protesting 'bout?" Immediately Sonya regretted the words. She imagined the old lady at somebody else's yard repeating what she said, making out how Sonya, the foreigner, distrusted her own daughter.

The old lady didn't answer Sonya's question but continued with the story the way she wanted to tell it.

"'Nuff people wan' leave Standfast, the country. But we never see anything like this here before. Nobody ever kill they pickney 'cause them wan' lef'. Nobody."

Sonya forced a series of yawns and rubbed her eyes.

"Yes, nighttime come quick," Maisey said as if she had only just noticed the darkness had crept in. "Get some sleep. Check you tomorrow."

Maisey shuffled off in the darkness. Sonya left the dark verandah and walked to the back, where her mother and daughter were grating sweet potatoes to make sweet potato pudding.

But the heat in the small kitchen stifled her. She left to unpack.

The rooms were as they had always been. Faded bedspreads brushed the floor. Empty perfume bottles took the place of decorative vases. In the corner of Kelithe's room, Timothy's toys lay as if he had just thrown them there: an upside-down truck, its wheels in the air; a small plane, with a plastic male astronaut sitting awkwardly on top of it; small Lego-like pieces fashioned into an unrecognizable object. There was also a pair of old sneakers, streaked with dirt, which Sonya remembered buying. One half of the bed was filled with Timothy's clothes and the other half turned down.

Sonya looked at the toys again, the bed prepared for night-time, and imagined her daughter was waiting for the baby's return. But Sonya wanted no duppies, no ghosts, to haunt the house. She looked for a crossed knife and fork, an open scissors, anything making the sign of the cross, an open Bible—things the old-timers have long practiced to keep spirits away.

"Kelithe!"

She fingered her daughter's things as she waited. She wasn't certain what she was looking for. The room was simply that, a bedroom. Except for the baby's toys, the room didn't imply anything about Kelithe's personality, didn't house any small things that suggested Kelithe liked to sew or read, hated cleaning, preferred one color over another. There were no hymnals or open Bible as in Grams's room, no books left over from her school days.

When Sonya walked through Kris's room, she looked for dirty clothes stashed away in corners, dirty cups or plates, inappropriate books, unfinished homework assignments, new toys or clothes her husband bought.

"How come you never turn the bed?"

"Turn the bed?" Kelithe wiped her hands on her skirt. Neither moved to narrow the space between, to make it easier for each to see the other in the lamplit room.

"Yes. To keep away Timothy's spirit?"

"He's my son," Kelithe said, simply.

"We turning the bed tonight. I don't want no duppy inside here wid me."

Kelithe moved from the doorway. "But he's my son," she muttered. "He's my son." She sat on the turned-down part of the bed, held the pillow to her breast, and bowed her head to it. "He's my son," she kept saying over and over—her voice hoarsened by tears—as if it were the answer to everything.

Grams came, though no one called her. She too stood at the door without a word.

Sonya turned quickly away from her daughter to her mother. "When Papa die, we turn the bed, the mattress. We sweep the floor. We lef' nothing out. And here you have the girl

74

setting up like she want the spirit to come. But I not sleeping wid no duppy in here."

"You don't have no heart." Grams walked away from Sonya.

"If is true what they say, that she just stan' there an' watch the baby drown—well, a baby that die like that going come back."

"Is still my house, this. And if she not ready to turn the bed, then we won't do it. An' if the duppy goin' come, is not you it goin' bother."

Sonya felt the shadow, the presence of a shadow, before she saw it. She was out in the early morning trying to summon the good news, wanting to be there waiting for the news from her God that everything would turn out all right. She wanted to find something to convince her the news she was hearing wasn't true. But her mother was up as early as Sonya was, and now stood behind her without a word.

Now Sonya wanted answers from her mother to the questions she had avoided asking—how the baby died, the reason for the roadblocks, whether her daughter watched. But she couldn't put together a question that seemed right, a question that reinforced her position as Kelithe's mother and Timothy's grandmother. She wanted a question that wouldn't read like an accusation if it were written down instead of toned down with a soft voice. She wanted to ask a question that reasserted her role as mother and grandmother, but nothing could rid their relationship of the absent years.

Her mother saw it before she did. The black crow sitting on the fence, wings spread and flapping so it could balance on the thin wire. She didn't think the word, the dark one everyone associated with a black john crow, but closed her eyes and waited for the news bug, or for something else.

Her mother bent and picked up a stone. "Nothing dead over 'ere," she said as she threw the stone at the bird. "Go look something dead."

Sonya closed her eyes on the last word. She didn't want that to be the last word she heard. She hadn't wanted to say the word at all or think it. A baby was already dead, and a town that wasn't used to fighting at all had blocked its only road and set fires as if the town residents were ready to revolt. No. She didn't want that sign at all. She wanted, instead, to associate the black john crow with something else, or else replace the image of it with that of a little brown news bug sitting on her arm and moving its wings in song. Good news.

If not good news, then nothing, no news. She simply wanted to enjoy the peace of the morning, the fresh valley air before the sun got going and spread its heat throughout.

"What the roadblocks for, Mama?" When she thought the question over, she didn't think it really came from her lips. It was simply one of the many questions she had played over and over in her mind.

"Roadblock?"

"Yes. The big fire out there, coming in from Cave Valley side. And the other little roadblock coming in from Orange Valley side."

Her mother kept her head toward the road, and Sonya wondered what she was looking for or afraid to turn around and say. She stood for a while looking out in the distance and rubbing her dry hands together. Sonya didn't like the sound her mother's hands made and would have asked her question again if her mother had not chosen that moment to bend down and pick up another small stone. She threw the second stone, but it didn't reach as far as the first one had. The hanging flesh on her arm shook weakly.

"I too ol' now to travel out the road dere. I only hear 'bout the roadblock. And it's one o' those things you have to see for yourself to believe. Nobody out here never raise a hand to ask for anything or join in anything goin' on roun' the country. So I don' know nothin' 'bout a roadblock. Can't tell you a thing."

"Kelithe never tell you? I sure she know 'bout it."

"Some things you have to see, and I too ol' for all that walking now."

"Maisey say everybody waiting to see what goin' come of the roadblock. Maisey never tell you all that? How come Maisey never tell you, Mama?"

"What Maisey know and what I know are two different things, you hear. Two different things. Maisey love run her mouth. Long time now. Anything you don't want to know and anything you want to know, she can tell you. She prob'ly can tell you things before it happen. But is I raise Kelithe, you hear? An' I know she wouldn' do a thing to hurt the baby boy."

Sonya wanted to believe her mother, but she knew that even if Kelithe hadn't told her, Maisey must have come and told her what was happening outside. Maisey had come last night even though Sonya hadn't yet been at her mother's house for a full day. She was as full of talk as she had been when she was younger, too ready to spread news. As small as Standfast was, not very much could remain a story between two people. Back when she was younger, people used to joke that news jumped fences to go to the house next door and didn't have to wait for anyone to carry it on.

Even if one thing in Standfast had changed, the way news traveled had not, and probably never would. And the odor of burning rubber was not a smell that would hover in a single place but one that would ride the waves of air and spread as far as it could. Burning garbage was an everyday thing, but the smell and the size of the fire from a roadblock were not. And even her mother, no matter how much she wanted, couldn't ignore the smoke that seemed to be blanketing the town like clouds, or ignore the whispers that had reached Sonya's ears the very night of her arrival.

Both Maisey and her mother's careful dance around the subject of the roadblock made her certain the protest concerned Kelithe, Timothy's death, and the story she had heard that Kelithe watched.

Now Sonya watched her mother's back and searched her mind for something else to say, for an authoritative voice to ask the other questions.

"How Kris and Anthony?" Her mother broke the quiet. "You never mention them at all."

"Fine, fine. Kris in the second grade now. Getting real big."

"Why you never bring her wid you? I goin' die before I get the chance to see my gran'chile."

"Too quick. Too quick to get everything together. Couldn't get enough money together so quick for the trip. But soon. Soon. I have pictures."

It worried Sonya that she had thought so little about Kris and Anthony, thinking so much about her dead grandson and her wish to be there now for the daughter for whom she had done so little before. But Kelithe didn't seem to need or want her, or maybe neither of them knew how to reach for the other through the years and years of separation. And she was having a hard time reaching inside for the motherly things she should be saying, or the mother's love that should cover, ignore, remove the little questions and the doubt that Maisey had planted like a little seed inside her heart and which had spread and blocked the prayers that wouldn't come out last night. She didn't want to doubt, wanted to think, instead, that the three-year-old had really just walked into the river and been overcome by the force of the water against his still baby feet.

"*The people saying she watch the baby drown to get her chance to go a foreign.*" She couldn't get Maisey's words out of her mind. They had formed their own little space next to the questions that had first come the morning after she heard, and went out onto her employers' balcony to look for a sign of good news to come.

"They block the road out so. And everybody watchin' and waitin' to see what goin' come nex'."

She remembered the quiet of the first day, her perception of the town lying in wait. And she wondered who were waiting and who were ready to burn the town, to show their protest with fires.

Now Sonya wanted to ask her mother more questions, to add to the single one her mother hadn't answered truthfully and find out what her mother was holding back—her mother, who hadn't kept anything back the first time Sonya had told her she wanted to go away, that she had filed the papers, and that someone abroad was helping her get everything together.

"And the chile?" had been her mother's question. "What about your chile?"

"I'll take her, too. As soon as I settle a little."

When the disapproval on her mother's face hadn't stretched into approval, Sonya had taken her mother to Montpelier, a bus ride away, to point out the things she couldn't get her daughter now that she would be able to get by going away. She had pointed to the nearby secondary school, the girls hanging out in the schoolyard with boys, neither group seeming interested in the learning going on inside the walls.

"That's not what I want for her, Mama. Is just for a little bit."

Sonya wanted an answer from that same questioning woman to smother the seeds of doubt growing faster and faster inside her and keeping her from reaching out to her firstborn daughter.

The "Good morning" came as a whisper from behind. Sonya returned the good wishes and turned her head slightly to look at Kelithe.

"Breakfas' ready now, ma'am."

Sonya looked back briefly to see that Kelithe was talking to her. She had been thinking so much, looking so far out into the distance, that she hadn't heard the sounds of a meal in progress, hadn't heard the banging of pots or hot oil sizzling or anything at all.

"Thanks. Coming."

Kelithe turned back through the house without another word. Sonya didn't make a move but kept her back to the house and her head to the street as if she were sniffing the air for news. She didn't move inside for breakfast.

"I sure you have pictures. Let me see." Grams turned away from her search of the empty roads and dropped her question as if it were a natural follow-up to a statement that had come before.

Sonya reached for the pictures, but she didn't move fast and she didn't move slow. It wasn't that she wanted to keep her life a secret. But there was so much empty space that pictures couldn't fill. She knew, because that's the way it felt with Kelithe.

"But she favor you though. The more she grow, the more she look like you."

Sonya watched her mother's fingers place the photos one after the other on her lap. Her eyes lingered for a long time on each photo as if she were memorizing every detail and etching specific features in a special place. Sonya, too, looked at the pictures fresh, looked at the floral couch in her crowded living room and thought of the hard chair in her mother's living room, the same chair that had been there when she was growing up, reupholstered once when she was small. She glossed over the remainder of the pictures after looking at one of Kris just as Kelithe walked back onto the verandah to ask her grandmother what she wanted for lunch.

"Look. Look on these, Kelithe. She favor her mother real bad now. Wasn't that way when she was little."

Kelithe took the pictures and looked at them with the same deep scrutiny.

"Big woman now. I remember when she was but so." Kelithe held her hand waist high, using the word "remember" even though she only knew her sister through pictures.

"Yes, she big now. Want to rule everybody."

81

It was their first real family moment, the first real conversation between Sonya and Kelithe.

Kelithe held on to the pictures, looking them over and over. Sonya wanted to move, wanted to see which pictures her daughter's eyes settled on—the baby pictures of Kris, her first day of school. She wanted to know if her daughter wondered whether there would have been, could have been, pictures like those of her.

She suddenly wanted to see pictures of Timothy, wanted to see for herself that her daughter couldn't have, wouldn't have, watched her child drown. She wanted to take her mind off her own failing, to put things back in perspective.

"You have pictures of Timothy?"

"Nothing else, ma'am. Jus' the ones on the walls. When he was but so." She held her hand below her waist. She raised her head slowly, after she finished saying the words, and looked into her mother's eyes. For the first time since Sonya had come.

Sonya moved her eyes down to the pictures Kelithe hadn't yet finished looking over and reached out her hands for them. Their fingers didn't touch.

"Kelithe?"

"Ma'am?"

"Don't call me ma'am," Sonya said. She looked up directly into her daughter's eyes. "I'm your mother. Don't call me ma'am like I'm some stranger to you."

"Yes."

# Sonya's Return

~

My mother wants Timothy dressed in a black suit. I want him in blue. That was his favorite color. And this was his favorite suit.

My mother comes back in a bustle to help me bury the grandson she didn't want, and didn't acknowledge until he was born. Her suitcases, boxes, and bags fill Grams's little house with her New York scent, and even though the windows are open and fresh air is blowing in, her perfumed sweetness still lingers in the air. A cloying sweetness. It is the scent of face powder and perfumed body powder. Perfumed body talc, the jar says. It is the sweet scent of a baby whose skin is covered with Johnson's baby powder, baby oil, and lotion, all three powder-fresh scents mingling. Overwhelming. The scent from the packets of air freshener that she sent years before, which I had stuck on the walls, never filled the house with their pack-aged floral scents nor lingered in the air like this.

She pulls the stiff black suit, still on the hangers from the store, tags hanging from the neck of the jacket, from among the things in her suitcase and, without a word about it, leaves it on my bed. She walks back across the hall to Grams's room and to her new things.

I hold the suit at arm's length to see if it would fit his body. Size three, the tag says. It's a size too small. He'd grown into a size four, and I'd begun to worry I was feeding him too much carbohydrates and meat with the fatty parts. He liked the skin of the chicken when it was fried crisp. "Scripsies," he called it.

My mother comes again into my room, new boys' shoes in her hand.

"What you doing?" This time she notices me hemming the legs of Timothy's pants. Even though he had outgrown the pants, I want to make them into shorts.

"You making baby clothes?" She looks down at the material in my hands, the scissors on the bed, the old slipper in which Grams stuck needles and dropped spools of thread.

"Just fixing Timothy burial suit."

"See the suit I lef' on your bed, dere?"

Even though I'd seen the suit, I glance toward it. There's also a package of boys' briefs. Three. He needs only one pair, but she bought a package of three. She brought black socks, too, and a matching clip-on tie.

"Yes, ma'am. This was his favorite." I don't tell her that the suit I'm hemming is the only piece of clothing I'd bought for him. Everything else he owned my mother had sent, either bought brand-new or collected from people whose children had outgrown the clothes.

Whenever Timothy knew we were going out, he reached for this sailor-type blue-and-white suit with its gold buttons. He liked the collar, and whenever he wore the outfit, he pretended he was transporting people. Only he blew his horn as if he were driving a bus, and called out, "One stop, driver," the way bus passengers do.

"What 'appen? You don't want it?"

"No. Is not that. I jus' want to finish sewing it. Since I start it a'ready. Maybe somebody else can use it."

"What, now you don't think the things I buy good enough? All this while I been sending clothes for the boy to wear, and he been wearing them? And now you goin' bury the chile in a suit that too small for his body? See the bran' new suit I buy dere an' you don' want it."

She grabs the suit as if she has to fight the bed to take it away, turns away with too much effort, stomping on the floor like a child. "Never see anything like this," she mumbles on her way out. Her jeans whisper from her legs rubbing against each other. She stomps out the back door, and from the window I see her talking to Grams, her hands up in the air as if she's batting away flies.

"Leave the girl," Grams says. "You never christen her in the dress I wanted her to wear."

I'm surprised Grams remembers that from so long ago, would even use that now against my mother.

"Better things for you to spend effort on. Don't worry 'bout the child's burial suit." Grams dismisses her with a wave of her hand and turns back to digging up the grass that has grown out of place between the concrete walkway. She's been doing a lot to get the place ready for the people she's sure will come.

My mother looks out of place here. Her jeans are faded above the knees, creased in the front as if she pressed them before she put them on. I know she wants to look relaxed, but it's not working. Her neon-green T-shirt is too bright next to Grams's faded floral housedress. Most of the buttons on Grams's housedress are missing. She closes the buttonholes with safety pins, some of the big yellow-headed pins we used long ago to hold Timothy's diapers together. Grams's brown socks don't match her old dress.

My mother's rubber slippers are too new, not yet dirty from the mud in the back of the yard. Her relaxed hair, without rollers, is too firmly curled, stiff with hair spray and small, tight curls, as if she just now stepped out of the hairdresser's shop and hasn't been here a day. Her eyebrows are arched, unnaturally thin; without eye makeup, they look as if they have been painted in place. If it were another time, it would be funny watching her, the prim and proper woman that is my mother, throwing whole grains of corn at the fowls and the yellow-fuzzed baby chicks.

There is no comparing me to her. I look like a younger version of Grams in a faded floral skirt and brown T-shirt. Underneath the T-shirt, my small breasts hang. The backs of my feet are caked with dirt because I have been wearing a broken-down pair of sneakers, and my legs look as if I wrote all over them with chalk. I keep my hair covered with a head-tie. Underneath, no curls. My hair is braided away from my face. The naturally curly and thick roots of my hair need to be straightened to match the straight ends.

But my mother bends over the coal stove as if it were only yesterday that she left here. The last time I saw her, she took me away from Westwood in a rented car without admitting that I was six months pregnant by a man she didn't know and a man I didn't know where to find. The car's air conditioner whispered the words that should have been spoken between us, humming a rhythm and blowing air colder than the winds that form over the Caribbean sea. I wanted to open the windows, but she preferred the unnatural air to the fresh island breeze.

Although we didn't speak about the baby, she sent boxes of baby clothes—old clothes in sizes from newborn to toddler that she collected from her friends' grandchildren and new clothes that she bought in discount stores—barrels of cereal, oatmeal, formula for the baby, and ten-pound bags of rice, tins of corned beef, and flour for Grams and me. Not a mother's love, but food to fatten the baby, clothes to keep him warm.

Now the whole town knows she has come. The rented Toyota she drove stands out front. The green license plates say RENTAL beneath the letters *RR* and numbers. I remember the softness, the comfort of the cushioned seats. I haven't been in the car, but I remember from long ago.

She came this time with boxes loaded in the half-open car trunk, tied down by rope. Her hard-backed blue suitcases lay on the car's backseat, two other boxes next to them.

When my mother comes back into her room, calm now, she calls Grams from the open window. Out of the suitcases and boxes, she pulls black funeral dresses for Grams and me. Black patent leather high-heeled shoes that I imagine sinking in the mud around the church and at the cemetery. Slips, brassieres, and panties. One large box, labeled "Twenty-seven-inch television," is loaded with bags of rice, flour, cornmeal, disposable plates, cups, spoons, knives, forks, napkins—stuff to feed the many who will come to mourn the baby with my mother and with Grams. Not with me.

"Kelithe, decide if you goin' to come back wid me so I can buy the plane ticket," my mother says through the doorway. Her voice is what my teachers at school would have called flat.

"Yes, ma'am." I'm never sure what to call her—Mummy, Mom, or ma'am. "Maybe I'll come up after the funeral. I'll prob'ly need a little more time to get things ready roun' here. And get somebody to stay wid Grams."

"You have anybody in min'?" She's shouting still, doesn't seem to notice that I've crossed the narrow hallway and am standing inside the doorway.

"Kin' of. Miss Maisey's daughter say she would do it, but she have a baby, so I don't know yet."

"Make sure she come by here before I leave so I can see her.

"Mama, I brought some other things for you," she calls again to Grams from the open window. "Come see if they fit you."

Grams takes her time coming into the room. She always walks slowly, never with a deliberate strut like that of a rooster. She holds up the black dress toward the sunlight slipping through the window and looks on the underside at the stitching. When she's done, she peels off her old housedress, taking her time to remove the pins and release the buttons, and is transformed in a black-and-white-print dress with buttons all the way down the front and two strings that tie into a little bow at the back. Grams's back suddenly seems straighter, and she smiles at her image in the mirror. My mother steps forward to close the buttons and look her mother over.

"Glad is the right size."

She looks over at me. "Try this, Kelithe." In her hand is a straight black dress with cap sleeves. The back dips toward the middle of my spine.

I'm suddenly conscious of my breasts, the hair under my arms, my slightly big stomach, my panties. When last had she seen me naked? Fifteen years ago. Then I had a body like Timothy's small one, without defining muscle and fat around my hips and waist, without stretch marks around my waist and hips, below my armpits. I feel now the same way I felt when the doctor came to the nurse's office and made me remove my clothes so he could determine how old my baby was and check its development. I felt exposed, acutely aware of the extent of my sins, and as dirty as if I were visiting an illegal bush doctor for a cure for a shameful disease.

I move to the corner, away from the mirror, and turn my back. My T-shirt goes first, and I drop the dress over my head and pull up the zip before I let the skirt fall around my ankles. I take my time adjusting the dress, look down at my hanging breasts, rounded stomach. When I turn around, my mother is still looking, standing still, and staring. I look at the transformed me in the mirror, and smile like Grams did at the new person staring back.

"It looks good," my mother said. "It was so hard trying to tell what kind of dress you would like. It's funny. I bought that for myself for a party. One time I wear it, and then it couldn't fit after that."

There is no price tag inside. Not like Grams's new one, which still smells like the store it came from. The dress my mother gives me holds the faint smell of her perfume and powder.

"Try this one too."

The second dress has a price tag hanging from the sleeve, and it holds a musty store smell. I step away from the mirror and turn my back again. When I turn around, my mother nods with pleasure. In the mirror, again, a new me.

"Here. Try the shoes." She holds out two pairs of patent leather heels.

Grams holds the shoes away from her body and looks hard at the heel. "Can't walk in that now. My days of wearing shoes like that over long time."

I try both pairs. I can feel the leather pressing against my toes, comfortably close.

"Thanks, ma'am." I leave the room, not wanting to undress under her gaze.

In my room, I look at myself again, imagine my body in the dress and my hair framed in different hairstyles. A new me. I want to smile again, but the circumstances for wearing this new dress and shoes, for showing off the new me, are not right.

I hold out the dress again, the panties, bras, slip, and other things my mother brought for me. I remember the things she sent me right after she left. The first thing was a doll, a chubby white doll with red hair and brown eyes. She had written in a letter to Grams, telling her to ask me if I preferred a doll with white or black hair, and I had said red because I didn't know anyone with white hair, except old people. I plaited the doll's hair, washed and twisted it until it didn't shine anymore and fell out in clumps. A foot and an arm fell off soon afterward, and the floral dress fell away, lost somewhere in the bushes around the house.

No matter how many things she sent, she had left me here, forgotten her soon-soon promise to come for me.

She didn't write to me often. She wrote mostly to Grams, always planning on what she would be sending next. I didn't write, just sent her the imprint of my flat foot and stubby toes via airmail for shoes that would come one or two sizes too big so I would grow into them. Grams and I measured our bodies, too, when we couldn't figure out our dress sizes. I remember measuring my bust, waiting for my first bra, waiting and happy that I wore a tunic to school, two layers of clothes, which covered the nubs that were my breasts.

Her love came in boxes, packaged as food and clothes and toys. Christmases and birthdays, and sometimes in between. Edible, wearable, seasonal love.

I don't know how to love her. I love Grams. I love Timothy. I loved Timothy. But my mother . . . I don't know. It's hard to love pictures, images that change each time she sends a new photo. When my mother first left, her hair was short. In the first picture that she sent her hair was straight, longer than I had ever seen it, and Grams said it was a wig. Her face, too, was different, powdered and smooth, her complexion looking lighter than it had ever looked. Each Christmas she sent pictures, mostly pictures of her in snow that looked like the cotton we used in Christmas plays at school. But her face changed, she changed, and when she sent her wedding picture, she was fat, round around the hips and with a lot of her breasts showing. Cleavage, everyone calls it. Too tight a dress, is what I say.

If that is how we measure love, then she loves me. But Grams loves me more. She stayed. Even when my mother was here, Grams did most of the things for me. She washed my uniforms twice a week so I would go to school clean, ironed my uniforms, stiffened the cloth with starch she made from cassava. She walked me to school, until I knew the way and could go by myself or with some older children from nearby. But not my mother. She bought my books, made sure I had a bag. But she didn't make my lunch, didn't make my breakfast before I went off to school in the morning or my dinner when I came back home from school in the evening.

I'm not sure if my mother loves me either. Love is not a thing we talk about. We love God, yes. We talk about our love for God, give ourselves over to him, open ourselves to receive his blessings and openly praise him for those blessings and whatever else will come. But we don't say, I love you, to each other. We measure love in what we do for each other, how much we spend or sacrifice.

I love Timothy. I stayed.

I wear my mother's love. I eat my mother's love.

# Three Generations
# of Romance

~

$\mathcal{L}$ ike the rolling calves and duppies the old-timers like to talk about, I walk at night. Without a bottle lamp filled with kerosene to light my way. All the familiar sounds don't sound so familiar anymore. Maybe it's because I'm aware of the beating of my heart. That internal rhythm throws off the crickets' song. What I hear, instead, is the song of frogs, and all I can imagine is their beady eyes and bumpy skin. Once I touched a frog, and it gave off a slimy mixture like saliva. Each time that day that I remembered the rough skin, I washed my hands, rubbed them with the hard scrubbing brush Grams sometimes used on mats and very dirty clothes. Frogs may be harmless, but a frog is the one thing I never want to meet in the nighttime. Certainly not tonight. A frog jumping in my way would make me scream and advertise to the women up ahead that I am here behind.

I slink into the back of the small peach-colored church for the revival meeting, into the whooping and hollering and praising. I cover my head with a black veil, blend in with the other women in the church. I sit in the back of the church, in a dark corner where the lights don't reach so no one can see my face.

The singing accompanied by shakers and cymbals, the warm-up stage, has come and gone already. And the pastor, loud in a purple robe, climbs the pulpit to look out on the others who're trying to reach his righteous height.

He clears his throat a little, thanks everyone, the large crowd that feels the pain of the lost boy, for coming out at night. He prays, too, that God may bless the soul of the lost and innocent child, the boy who was taken without even knowing that he was going somewhere.

"What kin' a country is this we living in? Ask yourself that, people." Beads of sweat are already pouring down Pastor Thomas's face. He wipes his forehead with a white handkerchief before shoving the rolled cloth back in his pocket.

"You all know what I'm talking 'bout. We living in a place where not even the police bother to investigate when a young boy drowns mysteriously. Yes, mysteriously. Ask the mother, and she will tell you that she didn't see or hear anything. A young boy, helpless, drowns in the river with his mother right there. She not crippled. She could have helped him. But our police don't even see anything wrong with that.

"The hospital, or what passes for a hospital out here, don't even do anything. 'It's a dead boy,' they said. 'Nothing you can do to save a dead boy, so just take the body to the funeral home.' That's the attitude. Nobody wants to take responsibility. The mother too young to take responsibility for her own child. So she kill him instead. I hear there is talk of obeah." He laughs a little, a high-pitched sound that doesn't seem to come from his round body. "Is always that we turn to. Our excuse for everything. But God is watching. He alone knows.

"This Thursday we bury that little boy. Timothy. We shouldn't have to. But we will."

I see Miss Rachael up front, nodding her head and mouthing "Amen." There are other faces I recognize, girls I went to primary school with, women whom I see in the market, on the street, women and men who are members of Grams's Baptist church. There's Teacher Williams's wife, who taught me at the infant school and who would have been Timothy's teacher if he had started school.

There's Miss Campbell, who came to Grams and said she didn't think I'd have the heart to do such a thing. "Is evil, the people, them evil. People never like see anybody else prosper. Always trying to pull another person down."

Grams nodded at her words, like an old woman with no strength left in her. And Miss Campbell went on, rehashing the good things she remembered about me as if she were writing my eulogy. She remembered the times I carried Grams's loads, how I helped the children studying for Common Entrance when I came home from high school for weekend breaks. She remembered the one time I testified in church, how afraid I seemed. But she's here with the others, sitting up front near the preacher, close enough to touch his purple robe.

Miss Maisey is also sitting up front. Next to her is my

mother. But my mother is sitting at the end of the pew, against the wall, hidden by the shadows of the bench. Her head is covered too, veiled like mine in black lace. I wish I could see her eyes, see if they are watering or if they are blank.

I don't know why I came here, what to imagine my mother will say or do if she sees that I followed her here.

The preacher wipes his brow again and holds his head down, as if he's forgotten what he intended to say. He takes his time turning the pages of the Bible. The room isn't quiet; there's paper rustling from the fans overhead, people turning the pages of their Bibles in anticipation of the section he'll read.

He rattles off the Ten Commandments, holding up a finger as he gets to the end of a verse. He repeats the ones that suit the night's purpose: Thou shalt not kill; Honor thy father and thy mother; Thou shalt not bear false witness against thy neighbor.

He repeats one a third time: Thou shalt not bear false witness against thy neighbor. "We're all sinners if what we saying isn't true."

For a minute he looks like a man thinking hard, the Bible against his chest and his head held down. "If it isn't true, and we all rising up, then, Standfast, Standfast, we're sinners in the eyes of God."

His words brought me a little hope. And I waited for something more, one person to say maybe I didn't do anything wrong.

The church shouts a collective "Amen," and a single voice says, "No, no, we not sinners."

"Truth. It sets you free."

It's a wide-ranging sermon, pulled from the Old Testament

96

and the New, newspapers and folklore. He goes on about love and responsibility, and it is this, it seems, the people want to hear. They're more vocal now, saying "Amen" and "Praise Jesus" at the end of every sentence.

"What is love? Remember the commandments. Love is in there. Honor thy father and thy mother. Love thy neighbor. Don't bear false witness."

He always manages to come back to one thing: truth. The *truth* he tells is the one my mother hears.

"Yes, God is watching, brothers and sisters. We can run, but we can't hide from the truth," the preacher says as I am leaving the church. I imagine all eyes on me. But it is too dark, and they can't tell who I am. And if they can, what does it matter? They all think I'm guilty anyhow.

I hold my head down and slink out the back of the church, the tears that hadn't come before flowing now from my eyes.

"You can run now. But you can't hide. No, brothers and sisters, you can't hide. You all remember the story of Jonah and the whale?" He laughs a little. "Even in the belly of the whale, he couldn't run from the truth."

I run.

What does he know about my love?

Mine is not a love story, not a story where my heart keeps pumping in anticipation of the next meeting with my lover. Nor is it a story from which daydreams, hopes, thoughts of marriage, come. It shouldn't be my story. It's a story about a quick rut under a coconut tree with a boy who has come back to his hometown to taste again the sweetness of country life before the hard concrete of the American city he calls home

97

stamps country lifestyle out of him. It's the story of a quickie that leaves a young girl pregnant, her onetime lover gone again to earn his keep in his borrowed home.

It was a time of waiting, waiting for the sun to go down so that my work would be over, waiting for the night to end, dawn on another day, to take me closer to September, when I would leave Standfast again. Waiting for my mother who had been gone for nine years to come back again, to fulfill her soon-soon promise. But the long nights of darkness couldn't be over soon enough. Standfast is dark at night, holding a dead weight that is sometimes lifted by church revivals, the heavy songs of praise that grab the night. But it was a slow time, then, slower when sitting at home with a grandmother who was too old to be a mother or a friend.

It's a story that many have heard told about someone else. A story whispered among girls at schools and ladies at churches, and held up as an example by guidance counselors and principals pushing students to reach for a little bit more than the older generation. A young girl who gets pregnant before she is ready, repeating her mother's, her grandmother's, mistakes. Not deliberately. Not because she knows no better.

It's not like Grams's story about her one love—meeting my grandfather for the first time as he stood under a coconut tree, a machete in his hand, his mouth still wet from coconut water. He had held the coconut out to her, empty of its sweet water, offering her the milky white jelly that she couldn't see through the small hole he had cut clean across the top.

She had giggled nervously at first, shaking her head, anxious for the opportunity to rest the heavy basket she carried balanced on her head and yet not wanting to appear too eager to stand there talking to a stranger. People talked, nosy old women who knew everybody's business and dropped words here and there, not knowing the full truth but dropping words with heavy meanings, hinting at one thing even though they knew it could be another.

"*I don' mean to carry any news, but I just see you daughta down the road wid a bwoy.*"

She must have thought too of her mother waiting at home for her to come back from the market with the food she had bought with the money earned from selling peas and yams. Waiting for the scallion or thyme or onions, or black pepper and salt she had bought from some of the other women who had also come to the market to exchange what they had for what they needed. Her mother waiting to season the meat and mix the flour for the dumplings to put on the fire. Waiting to feed the younger children who had earned their meal picking up stray eggs the fowls had laid around the yard and chasing the mongoose away from the baby chicks still walking around the coop. And they had been to school, learned their lessons for the day, and were ready now to rest their bodies before rising again at five o'clock to start the preparations and the journey to school.

But she had lingered anyway, talking to the boy with the too-dark skin, the boy that everyone must have called Darkey or Shine or some other name that always brought to the front of his mind the darkness and smoothness of his skin, the hatred they must have expected him to feel because of the common ancestry that circumstances had taught them to hate. She had talked to the boy, soon-to-be-man, with the cut-off khaki pants, his bare feet almost red from the dirt in which he had worked all day, planting yam and corn with his uncle and brothers, alternating between cutting canes with his father. She had lingered despite her thoughts that he needed a bath, needed to wash away the sweat that must have streaked through the dirt on his face as he worked out in the fields all day. She had lingered despite her anxiety, despite her thoughts that her father might come along the road with questions about what she was doing there, ready to beat the sixteen-year-old into obedience.

And then she had grown bolder, thinking of the soft jelly sliding down her parched throat, waiting for him to slice a small piece of the coconut husk for her to use as a spoon. And then to knock another coconut from the tree so she too could taste the sweet water. He had helped her lift the basket from her head, the basket that had been so heavy when she first saw him, even though she had been walking upright, swinging her hands by her side, just before she had come across him idling underneath the tree.

As she got bolder, she thought of the intimacy of sharing a coconut from which a stranger had just drunk the water.

"After me no wan' you mout' water. Pick another one give me," the suddenly bold girl said. She stared at his thin body, his strong legs straddling the rough but thin trunk of the coconut tree, his arms, strengthened by the constant use of pickaxes and machetes, reaching higher to pull his body closer to the bunch of coconuts. On his way down she memorized his face, noticed his dark eyebrows, thick but not overly so, and his eyes, which had probably earned him the nickname Saucer Eyes.

They sat together under the tree, their backs against the slim trunk, their legs stretched out before them, drinking in the coolness of the evening. From where they sat they couldn't see the setting sun, nor through the thick trees that branched out overhead, creating the look and feel of a forest. Even though she didn't know him, they had sat together, savoring the freshness of the coconut water, feeling the soft jelly slide down their throats.

But Grams only told me about meeting him, Joseph, under the coconut tree. Still, after six children she still remembered it, so I take it that the meeting, like their relationship, was special. The church wedding that came after their second child was born must have been special too, because she still had a single black-and-white photograph, hanging in a varnished wooden frame and tacked to the wall. She dusted it, too, much more regularly and with more attention than she gave the wooden clock my mother had sent to her.

Next to Grams's wedding picture is a Polaroid shot of Timothy, taken when he was three months old. The first picture of my baby boy, holding his head up and smiling a red-gummed toothless smile. An old friend of Grams who had come in from Kingston, driving a big truck and looking for land he said someone had been planting on illegally, took the picture, handing the still-wet paper to me. But there is no father standing by to round out the family picture. There is no Derek cooing baby words, encouraging his baby to hold his head up just a little bit longer for the picture.

Like my mother, and all the others who come every now and then, Timothy's father had come back to feel the August heat, to join the excitement around Independence Day and Reggae Sunsplash. I was home from school, waiting out the days, helping Grams feed the chickens, bring in the goats in the evenings, pull the peas out of the earth when the green pods had ripened to a red and light green or yellow. We shelled the peas and sifted the grains through sieves, separating the dirt and dust and doing it quickly before weevils hatched in the peas and spoiled most of the batch.

Mine is not a story that comes close to the sweetness of my mother's wedding, a wedding I didn't attend but experienced anyway because she sent a piece of her wedding cake, black fruit cake that had been soaked in rum, double-wrapped in wax paper, wrapped again in foil, and sent with a friend coming home. She had sent pictures, too, small glossy ones that mostly showed off the whiteness of the wedding gown that she had borrowed and worn simply for the pictures they had driven to Prospect Park to take, a wedding dress and train that hadn't swept the carpeted floor or brushed against the pews of a church. A veil, brushing her shoulders, that her husband, my stepfather—he wearing a borrowed tuxedo, complete with red cummerbund, that would have been too much for the chambers of a city hall judge—had not lifted to kiss her red lips and show possession of the woman now pronounced by the minister as his wife.

My mother had placed one of the pictures, a large full-length picture of her and her new husband, holding hands and looking into each other's eyes, in a frosted-glass frame. Grams kept the frame on her dresser, in the middle of the bottles of perfume and powder, which she never bothered to wear, and among the bottles of heart and pain medication that she always took. The other pictures, smaller ones, were in an album and were mostly taken in the small apartment, my mother and her new husband cutting the cake while their guests stood around the dining table.

They have a child, a sister I don't know. I've wondered what it was like for that second daughter. Did my mother love her from the first? From the moment she knew she was going to be a mother again? Did she sing to the baby in her womb, rub her stomach night and day? Did she hold her after she was born, place a finger inside the baby's powerful grasp, or rub my sister's soft hair? Did she fall asleep at nights with her baby lying on her chest, the way I slept most nights with Timothy? Did she spend hours trying to think of an unforgettable name, or did she think again of a way to end the baby's life before it began?

I don't know. But I know my story doesn't come close to my mother's romance. No. But it is close to the story of my mother and father, a father I saw once, long after he had been beaten and threatened with a cutlass by my grandfather. My grandfather, who had had two children with Grams before he bothered to receive the blessings of a church wedding, had chased and beaten the man who had come to tell him he had got his seventeen-year-old daughter pregnant. But he had come back, that thirty-year-old man, who had been chased off by a man about fifteen years his senior, had returned once, after my mother had run into him in Kingston—he had shown up to see what I looked like, to see if I favored him.

Mine is not a love story. I liked the way Derek talked. The Jamaican-American. Jamerican. The way he said "New York" with a smile. Flatbush, Crown Heights, the Bronx. Places of love. Places not standing fast. But places that carried dreams like eggs in a basket, gently so they wouldn't be broken or remain unfulfilled. Places my mother knew, maybe.

I liked the way he said his words quickly. Maybe. Not

maay-bee. The way he formed his words and sentences with care, the way our teachers taught us.

We practiced the way he talked. His twang, not my singsong. Because soon-soon, my mother had said.

"Sweetness," he said.

He didn't sound like the Jamaican men who shout "Baby," "Baby Love," from buses or trucks or yards, words thrown at almost every woman regardless of who she is or what she looks like.

"Sweetness," he whispered again from behind. When he said the word, I thought of a long-ago time when my mother called me Kel baby. Kelbaby. He sounded like my mother would have sounded if she had called me baby and come back to be my mother again. He sounded like love should sound.

I turned my head slowly, even though our guidance counselor had said ladies don't respond to such calls from men.

"Let me help you with your load." He caught up to me and took my plastic bag of groceries.

When I told him my name, he twirled it around his mouth and said it over and over like it was a magic word. He whispered it, drew it out, sang it.

He looked at my yellow summer dress with two straps tied at the shoulder. It was a new dress my mother had sent. I looked at his handsome face, his thick hair about as long as mine and pulled back in a ponytail, his thick cherry lips. He had a little hair on his chin. I smiled a little.

104

"I look funny?"

"Your beard remind me of a ram goat."

"All summer I trying to let it grow. If it don't grow, I'll shave it off."

His arms were big. When I looked at his bare arms, he said he lifted weights so he could play football at school.

"Football? What your arms have to do with kicking a ball?"

He chuckled. "American football. What you call football, we call soccer."

He walked with me nearly all the way home. I waved good-bye before we got there because I didn't want Grams to see.

When I saw him again, I was going to the river for an evening swim. He followed me there. He didn't splash water in my face the way Standfast's boys always did. He showed me how to swim underwater, how to hold my breath long and kick my legs like a frog. We went to the middle of the river and jumped off a rock. He watched me swim all the way across, with my head under the water, and not stopping to fill up my lungs with air.

When he joined me on the other side, he touched me with his hands. A feeling like the tickling of ants. It felt like love. It felt like the long-ago softness of my mother's touch; like Grams brushing my hair, parting and rubbing my scalp with oil. He made no promise. Just touched me. And I remembered love.

All evening I sang the Bob Marley song. "I don't want to wait in vain for your love." I remembered, too, my mother's promise and my long wait. He didn't promise. He didn't say "soon."

Derek didn't come back. Derek didn't know. Derek doesn't know that his son, born from the seed he had planted that evening at the river, drowned in the Rio Minho.

Mine is not a love story.

# My Mother's Love

It's surprising how easily it returns. Polite deference.

My mother comes into the kitchen, and I quickly raise my body from the kitchen stool. "Good morning, ma'am," I say, and stand there as if waiting for her to tell me to sit.

She looks like a brand-new doll with curled hair, not a strand out of place. A dark-skinned doll with perfect skin and clothes still stiff with spray from the store. Her perfume smells like a rose garden, strong but not overpowering.

She mutters her good-morning and goes about her business as if I'm not still here.

At school, we used to stand when adults entered the room and we waited patiently for their permission to sit. Walking on the steps, we stepped aside and let the adults pass as if their business were more important than ours. It's startling how quickly that mannerism returns to me. And sad. My attitude toward my mother should not be so formal. Even though I know I won't be punished for sitting without being told to, I remain standing and watch her moving around the kitchen.

She opens the covers on the pots. Cornmeal porridge cooked thick because that's the way Grams likes it. Fried dumplings on a plate with a pot cover over it to keep away the flies.

"Anything you want, ma'am?"

"No. No." She answers without looking back, as if she were programmed to say those words. It's as if only her body is here, moving without specific commands from her brain.

She takes a dumpling and returns the covers without sound.

"There's hot cocoa if you want."

I feel like I'm playing the "Mother May I?" game. I don't sit until she is outside the kitchen. The sound of her shoes fades to a single tap. Not long after, the car engine turns over, and Grams comes from her room.

"She gone to buy rice, as if she never bring enough."

Grams does what my mother did and checks the containers on the stove. She takes her own bowl of porridge and two dumplings. "She never eat the porridge?" Grams looks quickly at me, and I shake my head no.

"She never liked it from she was small. She like banana porridge. Or used to."

Alone again.

I want my mother's love.

I try to love her. Like I loved Timothy. Like Timothy loved me.

To get my mother back, I must lose my son.

Last night I fixed her bathwater, as warm as I used to make it for Timothy. The way she must have done for me so long ago. She didn't have to lift the basin either. I took it to the bathroom. And when she was done, I washed the tub down.

Tomorrow I'll do as Grams says and fix the porridge the way my mother likes. Not thick, lumpy cornmeal porridge. Smooth, creamy banana porridge. Nutmeg grated on top. Brown sugar sprinkled on top. That's the way Timothy liked it, too. With buttered hard-dough bread, the edges cut off. There's boiled bananas and ackee for lunch. Calalloo, if she doesn't want ackee. I'll make cabbage or corned beef. Whatever she wants. For dinner—pea soup or oxtail. Or something she hasn't had in a long time. Something I know she can't get over there.

She doesn't like Horlicks anymore. Timothy didn't like the malt drink either. But she drinks hot cocoa when Grams boils it, and warm Milo with lots of condensed milk when I make it.

Grams says she used to like bread pudding and sweet potato pone. And I remember how my mother used to break the bread into tiny bits or grate the bread fine and pour sweetened milk over it, mixing the bread to a lumpy, creamy batter. We ate the pudding hot, soft and squishy, almost all of it at once. When I find some time, I'll make some for her.

I peel cane for her and cut it into little pieces so she doesn't have to break it with her teeth. I give it to her in a bowl. I think that would be the American way.

I want to make a fire outside and set a Dutch pot to boil with curried goat meat, small flour dumplings, and potatoes.

Or oxtail with baked beans and rice. A big Jamaican meal to celebrate my mother's return.

She smiles at me, but she doesn't talk. For a long time I didn't remember her smile. I imagined she had a dimple. But it must just have been the way the skin on her cheek creased when she smiled. Or maybe it was the way she held her head when the photographer took the picture. I used to look at that picture every morning. One day it disappeared. Grams said she didn't know where I put it. I looked under the beds, on the dresser, in the kitchen cabinets, behind the living room couch, outside under the bushes. Days later I got tired of searching and stopped looking.

I'll do what she wants—iron, wash her clothes, part and oil her hair the way Grams used to do so long ago. After she left, Grams used to oil and plait my hair at night, and I would pretend I was my mother. Sometimes I would play with Grams's hair, pretending again that I was her. I know I can put the rollers in so she has tight, perfect curls.

I want her to call me Precious. When I was six, I called myself Precious because I dreamed that's what my mother would call me when I moved to that other country with her. "You're my precious burden," she would say when she brushed my hair and made it shine with Vaseline. Then she would rub a little bit of the Vaseline across my brows, smoothing them so they looked fuller.

That's what Grams did, anyway. And even though the Vaseline made my face oily, I didn't tell Grams to stop or that the children at school called me Shine, because I liked the feel of her hands on my face. I thought of Grams's hands as my mother's touch on my face.

I stay near my mother so I can hear when she calls. But my mother likes to walk. She walks the yard over and over. From the verandah to the yam hills in the back, to the grapefruit and orange trees, the rows of corn. To Papa's grave. Maybe she goes as far as Maisey's door. Her slippers are dusty now. Too much walking. I would go with her if she asked. For company. But she's always walking away from me.

I want her to stay and tell me of her other world. To fill in the spaces the articles and pictures in *National Geographic* and *Time* and *Newsweek* left blank. I want to tell her what I know, how much I have studied about America so that I could be close to her. I have pages and pages of notes on New York and Brooklyn, taken from three different sets of encyclopedias in the library at Westwood. I know the names of the fifty states and their capitals. The Manhattan Bridge and the Brooklyn Bridge join Manhattan and Brooklyn. Harlem, at one time the cultural capital for American blacks, run down now.

I spent my spare time in the library at school, learning those facts and making my dreams. Dreams of my mother coming to reclaim me. When I first started boarding school, I used to daydream about her searching the classrooms until she found me, even though the principal wouldn't have let her walk around the school like that. In those dreams she wore black and gold and dressed like an African queen and filled my classroom with her floral scents. Everybody looked at her and at me. I belonged to her.

110    But if ever she did come, the principal's office would send for me, and I would walk with a prefect or monitor, and none of the students looking on would know if I was in trouble or not.

That's not the way it was when my mother came. All the girls knew my sad story. And anyone looking from the classrooms saw a girl with her head down, her eyes on her rounded stomach, and a prefect walking straight-backed and holding the girl's hand as if she were weak. I held my head down when I saw my mother. She held her head high, looked down once at my stomach as if to confirm that what the principal and nurse had told her was indeed true.

She didn't ask anything. And I repackaged my dreams and my knowledge, keeping them, hopeful that another time would come when I could open them up for her.

Now, I am always near. She never needs to call. When she's ready, I will be here.

Grams wants the floor clean, rubbed with fresh polish, the walls wiped down, the furniture dusted, the yard swept up.

"People coming," she says as if she had a vision last night and saw the line of people making their way to the house. "Come, come. You sitting there daydreaming like you don't have things to do. A funeral to worry 'bout."

Grams hustles a way she never does. She searches for a dry coconut and carefully cuts the top part of the husk to serve as a brush so I can shine the polished floor. She even wipes the floor because she can do that standing up. I've never liked this part of housework—hands and knees on the floor, and carefully rubbing the polish into the wood with pieces of cloth. And over the same space again with the coconut brush, never letting up until there's a shine.

111

"What people coming, Grams?"

Last night I dreamed the women who followed me to the

funeral home were standing outside the gate. They were wearing white like ghosts, singing hymns, and swaying slightly. Their voices were soft, inviting. A part of me wanted to go closer to hear the comforting voices. Every now and then somebody whispered my name. They were waiting for me to come outside, to come to them at the gate, leave the protection of the house. In the dream, I stood at the window looking out and trying to decide why I shouldn't go toward the women. I turned around to slip a dress over my nightgown. But Grams was in the room. She, too, had heard the women calling my name. 'Don't answer and don't go," Grams said. She kept repeating that. When I jumped out of my sleep, I was too afraid to go to the window and look. What if they had been standing there?

"What you mean, 'What people'? Don't people always come round to the family's house after a funeral?"

"True, true," is all I say.

"Never yet see a funeral where the house not packed with people after the burial and the kitchen not overflowing with food."

# An Official Response

~

The river was as Sonya remembered it—full—and as calm and peaceful as Maisey said it had been the day Timothy drowned. Inviting. It was still too early for the women to be out, so there were no soapsuds clouding the water, no morning babble, no untended children sleeping or splashing around in the water.

Hardly eight o' clock when Sonya left the house, telling her mother she was going to buy some rice. She had brought more than enough, plus boxes of paper plates and plastic forks, seasoning, flour, to feed the people she had expected to crowd the house and mourn the baby's death. But she felt she needed an excuse to get out of the house alone. One day she had been there, and she felt crowded; crowded by the questions in her mind, the question in her daughter's eyes, the suspended promise that hung between her daughter and herself like a bridge that couldn't be crossed.

Mother and daughter flitted around each other. Sonya moved quickly, constantly, always conscious of Kelithe's slow, lingering movements; her daughter's watchful, waiting, questioning look, and eyes, round and liquid like a sun-warmed basin of water. It was a basin that Sonya wanted to see turned over. So she had spent her first full day walking. Not far, just around her mother's land, looking at the crops—the rows of corn; cocoa pods drying in the sun; ripe pears lying with their insides opened up to the sun.

Sonya remembered that Kelithe had always clung to her when she was young, wrapping dirty fingers in her skirt and burying her face when anyone spoke to her. "Handbag," some women had called Kelithe. And when Kelithe heard the word, her own pet name, she would slowly lift her eyes, looking out of one. She never smiled. Even when there were no strangers, Kelithe was always near, wanting to be touched, spoken to. Moments like those, Sonya felt closed in, very aware of the permanence of motherhood, how unlike a daytime job it was.

She stood on the bank of the river and pictured the women one more time, her daughter, her grandson, the tragedy. She wanted a happy ending to replace the sad part of the story that began right here.

But all she had in her mind was Maisey's voice. Sonya wanted something other than what Maisey had said. She wanted something other than what her mother wasn't saying, and what she hadn't asked and couldn't ask Kelithe. She just wanted to be certain, to have the facts laid out like a newspaper story: "Boy Drowns in Rio Minho"; "Police Call Boy's Drowning an Accident"; "Accidental Drowning Called Murder." Newspapers held the truth. Headlines blazoned across the *New York Post;* tacky, provocative, but some kind of truth. Those were the truths she was accustomed to. A policeman's word. An official statement. A coroner's report.

Sonya sometimes thought of the river as a place where answers would be washed up like mountain debris, but mostly she thought of it as a place where clothes were sometimes washed away, unrecoverable, and where promises were left in the air suspended like the once-new bridge that still swayed in the breeze waiting for an asphalt road on either end and a developer, public or private, to make it useful.

She remembered one promise given to her at the river. The *shush-shush* of the river. Frogs croaking. Crickets chirping. An orchestra accompanying his voice. Their bodies melding into the darkening evening.

"Bogle Princess," he called her, giving her his name as if it were the name of a tribe, and he the king of a people. She belonged.

"You'll be my African queen." Not a promise of marriage. But to a seventeen-year-old Sonya, being adored like a queen, worshiped and pampered, was more than any marriage could bring. More than her father gave her mother. A happy ending in the quiet, dying Standfast. But still a promise misread, worth less than it represented. The happy ending faded like the dust from his bike when he ran away from her father.

When nothing good came to mind, she thought of the deep brown Hudson River, its metallic smell, its movement made lazy by the dirt and secrets it carried. The children she watched in the day were fascinated by the Hudson River's

115

movement, only because they didn't see the filth, simply saw water and imagined the secrets beneath. If they could, they would watch the water for hours, picturing the swimming fish, waiting to see one jump up out of the water like cartoon fish, a shark with jaws wide open jumping after it. If any such thing could happen, the fish, Sonya knew, would be more likely to fear the pollution than they would a shark.

Sonya wondered if Jamaica's rivers, particularly the Rio Minho, could ever be so transformed. Even at the river's highest points, when it carried dirt washed down from the hills, the water was simply cloudy, never permanently stained. It didn't stink. It smelled of fish sometimes, a raw scent, but still fresh.

She looked at the stones glistening on the bed of the river, the luminous water, and picked up some of the smooth stones, sifted some of the sand through her hands. She wondered what Standfast would have been like now if the government had carried through its original promise of building a road through the town and funding the mining of the almost white sand and river stones. How many of Standfast's houses would have been concrete, with those same stones scattered on the verandah walls? Beautiful. Almost opulent. A contrast to the houses of wood and Spanish walls.

Sonya threw stones into the water, playing the varying plops over in her mind and watching droplets of water come alive. When she looked at the stones at the bottom of the river, she remembered the River Mumma story, a story Standfasters floated around as if it were theirs alone and not a folktale told in a number of different versions by most all Jamaicans. Sonya suspected that the people of Standfast held on to the story and made it their own because they, too, loved fairy-tale endings.

Perhaps Standfast's story would one day end that way, the riches of the river in hand.

The River Mumma, the mother of the river, had a golden comb. She had all the riches of the river, to give away to whomever she wanted. As the story goes, she used to come out early in the morning and sit on a rock, combing her hair with the golden comb that the river had made for her. She was rarely seen, but anyone who saw her would know that something good was going to happen. Most of the time she would give the person some of her riches from the river.

In Standfast's version, a boy named Johnny started going to the river early in the mornings just to see the River Mumma. He wanted to catch her comb because people always said that anyone who caught her comb and put it under his pillow would have a dream in which the woman of the river would tell him how to get more gold. He went often when it was still dark, sneaking out of the bed he shared with his brother. One morning when his mother sent him to catch some fish for breakfast, he heard a woman's sweet voice singing.

> *A me de River Mumma, A me de River Mumma*
> *Shwa, shwa, shwa, A me de River Mumma,*
> *A me de River Mumma, Shwa, shwa, shwa . . .*

When Johnny followed the voice, he saw the beautiful river woman sitting on a rock, her comb glistening in the weak morning sunlight.

"River Mumma," he called out.

The mother of the river jumped and dropped her comb. Johnny caught the comb and slipped it in his shirt. Still, he was frightened and ran back home to bed. He put the comb under his pillow. He dropped off to sleep and dreamt a song:

> *Bring back me comb, likkle boy, Me give you gol' and silver*
> *Bring back me comb, likkle boy, Bring back me comb . . .*

Johnny jumped out of his sleep and went back to the river. He heard the sweet voice again, pleading for her comb. But he didn't see the beautiful woman again, only heard her sweet singing voice. He threw back the comb, and as soon as he did he saw a pile of gold. He grabbed the pieces, dropped them in his bosom, and ran back home.

"A River Mumma give me," he shouted to everyone.

Nobody believed him. He carried his friends back to the river early in the morning, but from that day nobody ever saw the River Mumma again.

Sonya left the river before the women started coming, before anyone saw the car parked on the side of the road and started whispering.

After years of seeking happy endings, a fairy-tale ending wasn't what she sought now, but answers to questions to plug the hole that the constant flow of the river couldn't fill.

Sonya drove back the way she had come, squeezed past the still unlit roadblock, and took the near-empty road to the Orange Valley Police Station. She looked at the blue-and-white building, the officers in black pants, red cummerbunds, black-and-white-striped shirts, batons of honor and order by their sides.

Sonya sat in the car for a long time watching the officers

come and go. The post office to the left had just opened, and she parked there in front of the building, shuffling papers in her hand as if she were getting letters ready to be posted. The morning traffic rumbled by; busloads of school children; trucks carrying marl, lumber, bauxite; people heading to the market with and without produce. Very much the bustling town that Standfast had never managed to become.

Sonya simply wanted something concrete, more official than whispered words. She had watched her daughter from afar, looking for signs that Kelithe was mourning Timothy's death, anything that would convince her that Standfast's whispers were all lies. Only she didn't know what to look for, didn't really know whether or not her daughter would wear her emotions on the outside or keep them inside to be shared with a special person. She didn't know if her daughter had a boyfriend, if Kelithe had dreams like the ones she had had of leaving Standfast behind forever, if her daughter loved the simple life of the country town and never wanted to leave.

Things were different with Kris. Kris was an American child, demanding, outspoken, intent on being heard, whether she was right or wrong. When Kris cried, her entire body participated. Even though she was eight, she still stomped her feet, threw herself on her bed or on the couch and let her sobs flow through her body. She still cried in the supermarket or toy stores because she had sensed that embarrassment would push her parents to buy the things she demanded—dolls, taken from their plastic package and played with once or twice; a skipping rope that played a tune; sneakers that lit up like the ones her friends wore; shoes too high for her narrow feet.

119

But Sonya hadn't heard any crying from Kelithe. The nights were silent. She wanted to push for answers, but there were all those years in between, the presence of her mother, reminding her that she hadn't even been a part-time mother to her firstborn child.

"Mothering is a duty from God," Sonya remembered her mother saying, twice—first when Sonya searched for a way to stop the baby's heart that was beating inside her, with the hope that it would calm her father's anger; and second when she told her mother of her plans to go abroad and leave her five-year-old daughter behind.

"When a baby heart start beat, is not for you to stop it." Sonya brought her hand up to the place over her left breast where Grams had stabbed her with her finger that long-ago afternoon when they stood near the outhouse where Sonya had run after her father's beating. "This baby goin' born. You hear? It goin' to born and it goin' to live." Grams's promise was a threat. And even though Sonya didn't know what her mother would have done had she gone off and got rid of the baby, and even though she didn't know if her father's anger would grow as he watched her stomach round out, she kept the baby alive and watched her body spread into a mother's body.

For five years Grams's threatening promise and words about responsibility had held Sonya back. She watched her daughter grow while happy endings flew from her to be snatched up by someone else: *Manchester family seeks live-in helper to take care of two children in exchange for room, food and educational expenses. New hotel seeks domestic staff. American family seeks live-in helper to serve visitors at beach-side house.*

There was a family in Rio Bueno that Pastor Rawlings had pressed for her to go with. But she hid from him until he found someone else. When Sonya had first met the family, the man and his wife had spoken of a nearby community college as a place open to her. The woman—a teacher—had asked her to read from the newspaper and do some math, because shopping would be a part of her duties.

"Never mind, you'll get it," the woman said about the parts of the sentences where Sonya had failed. She seemed happy when Sonya missed something, as if the opportunity to mold an individual's life was more important than having a capable person to look after her children and keep her house.

But the eldest boy mouthed the words Sonya had missed. Sonya worried about taking care of children who knew more than she did. The children stared, too, their eyes crawling up from her dirty slippers, over her ashy legs, to her floral skirt and mismatched blouse, and to her face that she wasn't sure showed happiness at the opportunity or fear of the family and a life that was significantly different from hers.

All that time, she replayed her mother's words: "Your responsibility now is to your daughter." But Sonya viewed her daughter not as a gift from God but as a punishment her mother held up, a reminder of Sonya's failure, a reminder of the dream Sonya had shattered and the mistake she had known better than to make. Even though she thought of Kelithe, it was really the rude stares of the children and her fear that the older boy would always be asserting his superiority that made Sonya hide from the pastor.

When Sonya finally left Standfast, she left her mother's punishment behind. For those fifteen years, she viewed Kelithe

121

as a daughter—absent—and not as a burden holding her back. She pursued a dream, not necessarily a childhood dream, but something in a place that made her happy, a place that permitted an individual not simply to dream but to find an outlet for those dreams. Now, though, the burdened feeling returned; Kelithe was like a five-year-old, needy, questioning, persistently present.

Standfast, too, was simply too small for a woman who had been in New York for fifteen years, a woman accustomed to walking to a corner store to get ingredients for a complete meal; or driving to a mall to look at clothes she couldn't afford but hoped she could buy at a holiday sale; or stopping at a bookstore to leaf through magazines and soak up ways to remake herself and her life according to the latest styles. In Standfast, though, there was nothing to divert her attention from her adult daughter's watchfulness, the questions surrounding the baby's death, Maisey's persistence, her own mother's silence. Sonya wanted to hear one of her New York friends tell of the sadness of her married life, the husband who snored too loudly on the few nights he bothered to come home, or the sixteen-year-old girl who dressed for school in the morning but who had been caught twice at the Fulton Street shopping mall in downtown Brooklyn at midday. There was something comforting about listening to someone else's pain and offering advice that didn't mean much. It didn't matter to her whether her friends took her advice or not. Sonya simply enjoyed knowing that she had friends, that she was a part of a group, belonged in a small way to a community that could survive without her if she chose to leave.

The current situation presented a dilemma Sonya didn't

want. Standfast could make her an other, an outsider. Sonya will-fully forgot that had she succeeded in stopping the baby's heart that afternoon, nearly twenty years ago, she probably would have been on the wrong side of Standfast's anger. Perhaps that anger would have continued for the remainder of her time in Stand-fast. But she consoled herself by thinking that she hadn't carried out that act, and forgot that her mother's hand had been the pressure bearing down and preventing its completion.

Sonya longed to return to her day job. If the children cried, she held them till they stopped. If the little girl had a problem, she listened and told her to wait till her parents returned home from work, or wait till her mother called in the afternoon. Any-thing important enough that it couldn't be put off, Sonya han-dled. But those problems, insignificant or not, ended when Sonya left her job, entered the subway, and masked her face to resemble those around her. In the train, she observed the faces and bodies around, those persons who dressed as if they were successful, women who dressed like she did and probably watched other women's children in Manhattan apartments before going home to their own children.

Now that Sonya had returned, the five years she had spent trying to mother Kelithe rose up to her like a masked face in a dark, haunted house. Kelithe seemed to need her more than ever before, seemed to have picked up where the mother/daughter relationship had ended fifteen years before. Sonya wasn't certain what role was most appropriate—loving mother or grieving grandmother, or both. Her grieving daughter had questions in her eyes, craved attention and love. Her dead grandchild could ask no questions, needed no love, needed only to be dressed for burial.

The most she could do now as Kelithe's mother was try to clear her daughter's name.

None of the officers noticed the nearly new blue Toyota with the RR license plates.

From the police station, there were no sirens, no men sprinting down the whitewashed stairs into haphazardly parked cars. Some of the officers walked the verandah, tapping their batons against the wooden rail. Aimless. Purposeless. Like uniformed boys at a boarding school during their few free hours. Through the glass windows, opened as if they were welcoming doors, Sonya watched officers talking, laughing, eating. She didn't see papers shuffling or prisoners going in and out. Perhaps Sonya was too accustomed to the bustle of New York City, the ever-present ambulances, fire trucks, police cars. A city that demanded an unattainable order.

Only once had she been inside a police station. Anthony had been picked up and charged for driving on a suspended license. He had called and spoken to Kris, and Sonya had rushed to the police station, frantic, dragging the crying child who believed the officers wouldn't let her father out ever again but would bloody and bruise his face so he looked the way TV prisoners looked. It wasn't an experience Sonya wanted to remember. The police woman at the desk had treated her like the wife of any common criminal.

History repeated itself. The woman at the desk looked her over as if she were a common criminal.

"We have no record of the death," the officer said. Her lips barely moved. She looked up as if Sonya were an inconvenience.

"So there was no investigation?"

"Miss, we have no record," the officer repeated. She placed her breasts on the table, her hands folded in front of them.

"Who would have a record?" Sonya wanted her aggressive New Yorker stance, but her voice faltered on "record," and she looked away from the officer's eyes at the crucial moment.

"Where is the body, miss?"

"The funeral home."

"Try them. Maybe they can help."

"But some people say it was murder. How come you don't know?"

"Miss, we have no record. If we have no record, it wasn't reported. Do you want to make a statement?"

Sonya faltered. She had only wanted an answer, to know for certain if what Standfast was saying was true. Making an unsubstantiated statement against her daughter was another thing. Unethical? Wrong? She looked behind the desk at the officers laughing. There was no order, no filing cabinets, no computers. She thought of her statement getting lost some- where, or perhaps being filed away neatly in the offices farther back, a summons for her to testify against her daughter. But what did she know? The absolute truth? No. What she had was just Maisey's words, two roadblocks, and a protest without conviction.

Sonya brushed her clothes down and left. She stopped at the bottom of the whitewashed steps, looked back at the white building, the blue paint ringing the wooden shutters.

When Sonya left the station, she looked down the street toward the corner drugstore, across at the post office, the Peo- ple's National Bank, hoping she didn't see a familiar face.

If anybody had asked, Sonya wouldn't have been able to

recall anything of the drive from Orange Valley. She didn't pay attention to any of the developments that had sprouted in the fifteen years since she had left. Nor did she stop at the funeral home to view the body of her grandson, inquire about the death certificate, or settle the funeral arrangements as her mother had asked.

She repeated the officer's questions, rearranging her answers to better suit an aggressive New Yorker. She should have demanded to see the woman's superior. Should have threatened to write a letter to the commissioner of police, the governor general, her member of Parliament. But that was the New York way, not Standfast's, and Sonya didn't want to upset the accepted ways of things. Standfast viewed her as a foreigner, regardless of where she had been born and raised. She had left, had prospered, would never anymore be satisfied with washing her clothes in the river, beating clothes against rocks, catching, killing, and pulling feathers from a chicken, cooking on a coal stove, doing for herself, and not asking for an outsider's help. She was a New Yorker. She had come to take her daughter.

If anybody had asked, Sonya wouldn't have been able to say she had had those thoughts. She remembered nothing.

But she definitely heard the boom and saw the children running from the side of a wood house. A few children ducked. Others stood boldly, defiant. When she felt the car jolt, the steering wheel slipped under her hand. She forced herself to right the car, to look, to comprehend, to remember. Their feet were dirty, a red-brown. But what good would such a description serve? She didn't see their faces, couldn't tell if any had broad noses, thin lips, high foreheads, crooked teeth. Nothing.

She slowed the car, looked through the rearview mirror. The crack in the back window spiraled out like cobwebs.

She thought the children barked, "Murderer," branded her with a name. She couldn't be certain because the air conditioner was buzzing; the comfortable car was designed to cushion her against unwanted outdoor noises. So the car manufacturer's papers said.

"Lord Jesus."

Sonya looked around to determine where she was. Standfast. Near Teacher Williams's school.

She saw the second stone coming directly at the windshield, felt sweat dripping between her breasts, pee straining her bladder, and wondered if that was what the john crow she had seen the second day after her arrival had meant—her death, not the baby's, not Kelithe's. She cracked her knuckles, bending the fingers on her right hand first, then her left. She stopped the car and waited, imagined her husband's face, pictured the photo of her, Kris, and Anthony, taken at Coney Island beside the Wonder Wheel. She looked at the picture each morning when she woke. Happy faces, pleasant memories. That's what she wanted to think of when she died. Sonya pressed her forehead against the steering wheel, careful not to let the full blast of the horn wake the absent adults. She shuttered her eyes and waited for the glass to shatter, the splinters to pierce her skin.

So carefully she had walked the streets of Brooklyn, maneuvered around Manhattan. Home by five in the winter, just when the oppressive dark was bearing down. Never on the street after 8:00 P.M., as if eight o'clock was a magic number that summoned crooks, thieves, rapists, New York's evil. Kris

127

knew her rules. Her husband made his own. Still, she was from Standfast; she avoided trouble.

"No look fi trouble; mek trouble come to you," her mother used to recite like a mantra. At the end of those words was a warning of a potential beating with a tree limb or a hastily grabbed shoe.

She jumped when she heard the pop, waited a moment before she looked between her fingers at the second cobweb.

The children laughed. Ran. Sonya looked again, wanting to notice distinct details. That's what detectives always wanted. Specifics. A man with a red shirt, goatee, was seen running away from the scene. She remembered but couldn't focus through the shattered glass. She saw adults running toward the car, a few men with machetes in their hands.

"Mi God," she said. "Standfast. Standfast?"

Sonya started the car and drove. She bent forward and leaned a little to the right so she could look through a clear part of the glass. She didn't think of avoiding the holes in the road. Once she looked back and through the dust saw the men and children standing still, a very old man in front, his back turned to the car, his arms waving at the others to stop.

"Look what the blasted people dem do!" Sonya shouted from outside the house, her voice near breaking. Dust billowed around the car like a curtain. "Just look dere."

When Grams rose from the lightweight lawn chair, it wobbled. Grams held on to her cane, stepped down the single step from the verandah to the walkway.

"Kelithe! Kelithe, come quick."

Sonya pointed to the shattered windshield. Sunlight

reflected off broken pieces of glass on the backseat. Grams touched Sonya's cheek, felt her head for bruises.

"You not bleeding?" Grams asked. "What happen?"

"Children. Children fling rock stone at the car and run."

Sonya looked at Kelithe as she explained what happened; her eyes gazed directly into her daughter's, unwavering. Kelithe looked back, her stare as strong as her mother's.

"All the money I put down as insurance for this car gone just like that." Sonya didn't look away from Kelithe. "And for what?"

Sonya didn't ask Kelithe what had happened that Thursday afternoon when Timothy drowned. She simply accused her daughter with her stare. She looked again at the car. She shifted her gaze momentarily to the house, which remained achingly similar to all the houses in Standfast despite all the money she had sent over the years to fix the roof, add a room for Timothy, attach a bathroom to the side of the house. The house was as it was when she lived in it. The outside walls had never been painted, and the gray concrete mirrored the darkening sky. The flower garden was clean, tended, but sparse; the flowers bloomed one by one, and were mostly withered. She looked at a lone pink anthurium, out of place, unprotected.

Once more Sonya looked at Kelithe, her stare hard, challenging. Kelithe looked back, her stare soft, questioning. Sonya looked away. Fiery anger she could handle, but not eyes that asked questions and a body that wanted her touch. She thought a touch signaled a promise she wasn't sure she could keep if what the town was saying turned out to be true. And she wondered, if the stories about Kelithe weren't true, if Standfast's children would have shattered her car like that.

129

Even if Standfast's words were true and Kelithe was indeed guilty, what right had Sonya, who had nearly aborted her daughter at the first sign of her father's anger, to point a finger? What right had she, who abandoned all motherly responsibilities, who had a daughter she barely knew and one she preferred not to know at all, to judge Kelithe's action or lack of action? Although Sonya glimpsed a shadow of her desperate self in what she thought of sometimes as Kelithe's desperate action, she consoled herself by thinking that she had not fulfilled her initial impulse to abort the fetus. She brought both her babies to term. She mothered her firstborn as long as she could. She was still a mother to her secondborn.

For the first time since Sonya's return, she thought of herself as a child again, pushing her mind to envision the fairy-tale ending. The departure she envisioned was the direct opposite of her coming. Throngs of people gathered to wave her car away, and words of kindness tumbled from their lips. Kelithe was there beside her, also a recipient of the kind words. She saw herself walking through U.S. Customs, her daughter behind her, and into the open arms of her husband and secondborn.

Sonya warmed her own bathwater, waved Kelithe and her mother away and leveled the bucket over the fire. She took the basin of water into the bathroom herself and didn't think once about the inconvenience of having a bathroom with a bath and no running water. When she had had the bathroom built, she had told her mother to look for a place for a tank to be built so they could pump water into the house. Her mother had said no because she wanted to consider the neighbors who didn't have and perhaps would never have the same.

Sonya didn't stay long in the tub. She had never been a person for long baths. When she finished, she scrubbed the tub herself. She went to her room, wrapped her hair, and settled to wait for sleep.

"Dinner ready now, ma'am," Kelithe said outside the door. Her daughter hadn't bothered to knock or announce her presence.

"Okay."

Sonya didn't touch the meal her daughter had cooked. Not once did she look at the pea soup she smelled, or think of the soup bones she loved to suck for the sweet meat. Instead, Sonya took the seeds from some ackees her mother had in the kitchen, soaked some salt fish, and mixed her flour for dumplings. Grams hovered over Sonya, took a knife, and helped to deseed the ackees.

Kelithe lingered in the shadows, watched her mother, and waited.

They didn't talk, but Grams sang "Swing Low, Sweet Chariot," over and over again. Every now and then she wiped her eyes when the tears, falling from her remembering Timothy, were too much. Grams sang while Sonya cooked.

"He's gone to his maker," Grams said over and over, as if those words were enough, or what Sonya wanted to hear.

"What you more upset about, the car or your daughter?" Grams asked when Sonya finished her meal. "I raise you, and I raise Kelithe. None different. What make you think she would kill her chile? What give you the right to believe them?"

Sonya didn't answer, perhaps wasn't even aware of her mother sitting there and her daughter standing in the shadows, still waiting. She washed her plates, made her cocoa.

"Who you goin' believe? You' own mother or everybody else?"

"Is one story I hear." At last Sonya looked at her mother. She raised her voice a notch above her mother's. "I ask you what the roadblock for. You say you don't know anything 'bout a roadblock. You the adult. You the one I ask. The car out there with the glass crack. If the children did throw the stone a little harder, it could have hit me. What you goin' tell me 'bout that? Eh?"

Sonya waited for an answer, watched the surprise on her mother's face disappear, change to anger.

"Six children I raise. Six. You the last. Then Kelithe. Not one of them, all older than you, ever talk to me that way. Never. The others all gone now. You and Kelithe the only ones I call my children. Kelithe don't treat me that way."

"One baby dead a'ready. And you can' give me no answer. When you goin' tell me? When stone hit me and I gone, too? What you have to hide?"

Grams left the room, passed Kelithe standing in the shadow, and closed her bedroom door.

Sonya's own conscience, the guilt she felt at leaving her daughter so long, should have made her want to scurry away with her daughter during Standfast's starlit and candlelit night. But she was certain Kelithe would resent that idea, resent her for implying that her daughter was guilty. Sonya worried as well about what the townspeople would think of her, how their opinion of her as a dutiful mother who had come to support her daughter would shift to that of a mother who helped her daughter escape justice.

The Standfast instinct to wait crept back in her. Sonya took the warm cocoa to the verandah to watch and wait. But that she couldn't do. Not quite regretting the unpleasant exchange with her mother, Sonya left the house with a high-beam flashlight she didn't turn on at first. Her white dress fluttered in the breeze. Her sandals clomped over the stones. Had the sky been filled with a full moon, someone would have mistaken her for a duppy, a ghost. Or maybe a rolling calf because of the noise her shoes made.

She remembered a childhood belief: Drop pebbles when you walk at night to keep the ghosts away. Ghosts, her mother said, couldn't count past three. "One, two, three." Once the duppy got to three, he would have to start over again and again and again. And she would be free. Sonya dropped pebbles now, not quite certain why she was out there. As dark as the road was, she feared it less than she did New York's streets. Sudden noises could make her heart beat faster, make her walk faster or run a little, but the scare wouldn't amount to more than that.

When she got to Maisey's house, she saw a light from the front room. She tapped lightly on the door and held the flashlight so Maisey could see her face.

"Sonya? Is late now, you know?"

"Jus' tek a little walk. Like old times."

"Sorry 'bout you' car. Children sometimes try every bit of patience."

"Somehow I don't think is them alone wish me that bad luck. Everybody have it out for me." Sonya swallowed hard. "And Kelithe," she tacked on belatedly.

They ignored time, the lapses of conversation between them, the nighttime quiet. There was nothing besides Standfast's action that they could discuss, without the subject appearing to be a blatant replacement for something else. So

133

when the conversation lapsed, they simply waited out the break and started up again as if their talk had been continuous.

"Mama telling me one thing. Kelithe not saying nothin'. You telling me something else, and Standfast acting like the girl commit bloody murder. The roadblock, the stones they fling at the car. With all that, I don't know what to think."

"In all my seventy-odd years, these people never do this before. So I would tell you, go wid your gut feeling. Is late now. I will walk wid you part way."

As Maisey spoke, she rolled sheets of newspaper and pushed the wad down into the small neck of a beer bottle so it touched the kerosene in the bottle. She touched it lightly with a match, watched the flame rise, and handed the small bottle to Sonya.

"Careful now."

# Wait, and It Shall Come

~

*T*his, too, I would have told my mother if she had asked. But I tell it to the men instead. They come at dusk. Almost as soon as the car stops and the circle of lights go out, it is pitch-black, as if they carried the night with them. When she hears the crunch of gravel, not because of the car but from the weight of the men's steps, my mother takes her cocoa and hurries inside.

"Somebody out there to you," she says to Grams as she passes through the living room.

Grams calls me away from the dining table. I have no time to wash the meat grease from my hands but wipe my fingers in my skirt so my hands, at least, will be presentable.

Father Rattray hugs me as if I am his lost daughter. And in a way I am. He called all the girls at school his children, and when he led morning prayers, he asked God to "keep our daughters in your fold."

"The Lord is with you," Father Rattray says.

It must be what he says to all the mothers he comforts. And maybe the children as well.

He's a short man who lost his hair too quickly. He has quick eyes and, according to the night whispers of the girls at school, quick hands too. He has a wife, who, next to him, looks too tall. She always fed the girls in the Methodist Youth Group Danish butter cookies and too-sweet juice—sometimes guava, sometimes pineapple, every once in a while tamarind or thick cherry juice—whenever we met at her house for meetings. The girls always had a story to whisper about him, but they never said anything about his wife, who spoke with a young girl's voice and walked on the tips of her toes like a dancer.

I liked her. When I thought of myself as a full-grown lady, I imagined myself like her—poised, with a perfectly placed hat on Sundays and neatly curled hair the remaining six days of the week. When she spoke, her lips didn't seem to move, and she never raised her voice. In her presence, I always thought of the word "intimate," because she moved in so close to anyone she was speaking to and spoke so softly that she always seemed to be telling a secret. And she touched. No matter what the conversation, she touched the person she was speaking with, either a hand on the shoulder or back or a quick brush with her palm on the hand. Soft hands. The direct opposite of Grams's work hands, made rough by hoeing and planting and pulling peas out of the ground. She spoke the way our principal said we girls should—the Queen's English.

Father Rattray, the girls said, should never have been a

preacher. His calling must have been a mistake; he was too worldly, knew too much about music and the Hollywood lives of musicians, the books we girls liked to read at night with flashlights, the fashions we wished we could wear instead of our uniforms. Second, his shoes. Always with too much heel for a man. Some joked he was trying to catch up to his wife's height. Others thought, but no one said out loud, that perhaps he was effeminate.

My long-lost "father" comes with the new minister from the Methodist church near Orange Valley. I never learned his name. Once, I sat in on one of his services. But I didn't like his voice, the way he squinted when he looked down from the pulpit, nor how quick he was to notice I had never been there before. At the end of the service, when he called for first-time visitors to stand, he coaxed and coaxed until I stood up with my baby in my arms. I felt all the eyes on my young face, Timothy's smiling face, and imagined the thoughts churning in the minds of the Christians. I never went back.

"I think you know Reverend Morris," Father Rattray says.

Reverend Morris's hand is cool when I shake it, not clammy-cool but as cold as hands that have been on ice. I've heard he gets involved in political causes, raising money for one candidate or another, telling his church to support one candidate and not the other, calling the radio stations to debate just punishment for criminals. I understand why he is the one to bring Father Rattray.

Reverend Morris, too, says something I think he says to all the people he comforts. "God doesn't owe us any explanation, but when he sees fit to make us understand, everything will be clear. One day you will understand. Or you may never understand. Some things are not for us to understand."

I point to two chairs. Grams brings a lamp that I set on the floor between us as if it is a dish we will each dip into. She shakes both their hands, thanks them for coming, and steps back into the dim house. They apologize for the hour they've come, but I wave the apology away as if I'm accustomed to having visitors drop in at all hours. Why should they know they are the only visitors I've had? I offer them the papaya juice I had made for my mother, and they swallow the liquid as if it's the only thing they have had to drink all day.

"We came because we thought you might want to talk," Father Rattray says. "We heard . . ."

He doesn't say rumors, or stories, or news. His opening sounds like what he said once before. "I heard . . ." Three unspoken words: . . . you were pregnant.

He was one of the few adults who spoke to me during that last week at school when I waited for my mother to come. During the daytime, I was confined to the nurse's office as if I had TB. I knew then how Michelle Redway had felt when she was kept in the nurse's office because she had a deep cough and sputum that made the nurse suspect TB. Brown-uniformed public health nurses came and gave a little needle stick in the arm to test if all students had received the TB vaccine. Each of those five days that I sat there as if I had a contagious disease, Father Rattray came. He didn't then speak about God or Christian values, but mentioned hope and love and dreams and goals as the things that keep people from dying on the inside.

"Don't let this baby mark the end of your dreams," he said.

138

If only he had known how little my dreams depended on me and how much on my mother keeping her promise.

They sit expectantly, Father Rattray with his hands in his lap, one palm upturned as if it were holding something soft, or waiting for something soft. That's the way he sat when he came to visit me at school. So I tell them a part of my story, what I would have told my mother if she had asked.

*Grams used to tell me, if I looked too hard, she would never come. If I looked everywhere for the needle, I'd never find it. If I looked for the book, I'd never find it, but it would turn up in a place I never thought to look because I didn't expect it to be there. But when I stopped looking and didn't need it anymore or found something else to replace it, I would find it. It would appear. Just like that.*

The lamplight shows half their faces, Father Rattray's dark, shiny forehead. I don't look at them because if I did, I would probably stop. I think of Mr. Brown's Speech and Drama class, the way he made us girls stand on the stage without fidgeting, without moving our feet in nervousness or twisting our hands in our skirts. I think of myself in a pressed blue tunic and white blouse, gleaming black shoes, on a stage in Kingston or Mandeville or Montego Bay, or at a hotel in Negril reciting a poem for tourists. The one lady chosen to represent the school at the annual festival. The tactic makes me go on. That and my belief that their eyes are kind.

*Grams used to say that a person shouldn't look for love. If I looked, I'd find the wrong kind. Love just came. It wasn't* something to find. I'd meet a man, a good husband. He was not someone to find. Wait.

I kept one pair of good panties with elastic in the waist and legs. White. One good slip. Black. A bra. Not too tight. White. A dress without holes. Not faded. Not stylish. Blue. Money for stockings. Just in case. The shoes, though, would worry me; they were all broken, dirty.

Wait.

For Timothy I did the same. A good shirt and pants. Starched and ironed. One pair of white briefs. Polished shoes. We waited and were ready. Just in case.

No suitcases though. We wouldn't need what we had.

Passports. Birth papers. Timothy's favorite books.

Jamaican food—roasted breadfruit, ackee, peppers, cut cane, pears, hard-dough bread. Those could be prepared quickly. It's the food I would miss most. And Grams. But my mother manages without the food. She must have found something better, or maybe she gets some of these things there. Star apples. Guineps. Naseberries.

It's not that I don't love Grams. That's not why I watched and waited. I waited because soon-soon, my mother had said. I watched because my mother pointed to the sky and said America. America must be a place like heaven. In her pictures, she stands in snow that is like clouds. If I fall in the cloudy snow, I won't be hurt.

I waited because Papa didn't leave Grams when he died. He said he would wait for her on the other side. He, too, is waiting. She said she would see him on the other side. You don't leave the one you love. If you leave for a short while, you must return. So I've always known my mother will come.

*Fifteen years of watching and waiting. A long delay because I watched and waited, looked too hard down the dirt road and up at the sky at planes. When my mother sent the picture of her new husband, I counted out the things I would carry. She was no longer alone, so everything should be better. I waited. When she sent a picture of her new baby girl, I packed the things I would carry because her situation certainly was better if she could have and keep a new baby girl. When she sent money for Grams to build the bathroom, I said tomorrow. Tomorrow for sure. I waited.*

*There was a girl at school. Celia. Her mother sent her back to Jamaica for school. She flew back to America for Christmas and at the summer break. Once I remember she went for the five days of Easter break. On fourth weekends she went to her grandmother's house. And I dreamed that my mother might have been like Celia's mother. A part-time mother. At least.*

*Without warning she sent a letter. "I'm ready. Things much better now."*

*Fifteen years.*

*I've been ready, Mom. I want to call her Mom. I've practiced calling her Mom, the way some of the girls at school used to do. "My mom," they said. Mommy. I like the sound of the word. Before she left I used to call her Mummy. Then I found out that's what they called the dead in some countries. Sometimes I called her Sonya, repeating what Grams and everyone else called her. She didn't mind. Sometimes she never heard me at all. Grams said she was daydreaming. Sometimes she looked to the sky, and I thought she was praying.*

Later she pointed to the sky and said, "I'm going to America. Just for a little while. Soon. Soon you can come and be with me there." She had always been daydreaming of her heaven.

What would I call him? Dad? Daddy?

My sister, Kris.

I've practiced speaking like Mom now speaks, the way Derek spoke. American. Good English.

"Enunciate," my teachers said. "Do not eat your H's. Hit. Not 'it.'"

Once I read a Bible lesson at a Christmas program. I wanted my mother to be there. To hear me speak. To see me on a stage in front of a crowd of people.

At nights I read the Bible out loud. Carefully. As carefully as the newsmen and women on the radio, as precisely as Principal Pinnock. If I had a recorder I would tape myself. Play it over and over. Make the words right. I've wanted to ask her for one, tell her I was practicing good English so I would be ready when the right time came. I didn't know what she would say. I never asked.

"I'm ready," she said. Fifteen years. Fifteen years I waited to rest my mother's soon-soon promise. "You have to leave the baby for now."

No. I couldn't leave my son with a bottomless promise.

My mother's promise is half my life. Soon. Wait. Fifteen years.

142

My son is the other half. Three years. An education ended.

"Dream" is a word I once knew. I want to be . . . All the world stretched out, displayed like the cakes we baked in

*Home Ec. Some round and brown. Others sunken because
cold air was allowed into the hot oven.*

  *My own promise suspended. What now? Standfast. Stand
fast?*

This is my story. My prose poem. The waiting I didn't want
my son to know. Ever. How I didn't want to leave Timothy
because I loved him. I don't tell them this part, but it is what I
want them to understand. What I want everyone to understand. Neither my mother nor Standfast has listened.

They are silent. Father Rattray's hand is still upturned. He
is still waiting for that precious, soft thing. He glances briefly at
his partner and stretches one hand toward him, the other hand
to me.

"Let us pray," he begins, as if he is talking to a hall full of
people. "Our father who art in heaven . . ."

It's been a long time since I've prayed. And surprisingly,
not since Timothy's death. Crying has been easy, but not
prayer. What I want is the return of my son, and that sort of
miracle will never happen. There might be miracles elsewhere—a statue of the Virgin Mary crying, a patient thought
to be dying of cancer but who survives years beyond all doc-
tors' expectations—but Standfast has never had a miracle,
and I don't expect one now. I used to pray a lot. Night and
day I prayed for my mother's return, or if not, a fulfillment
of her soon-soon promise. But there must have been a pact I
was never told of—my son for the beginning of my life elsewhere. If I had known, I would have stopped asking a long
time ago.

Inside a door slams shut. The noise is so sudden it reminds

143

me of a quick splatter of something, perhaps a dead bird falling after being hit with a stone from a slingshot.

The Lord's Prayer is the only one he says. Somehow, I had expected him to lay his palm on my forehead and give me a needed blessing. Reverend Morris doesn't pray for me at all. He must think there is no hope.

They don't linger. Besides holding my hand during the prayer, neither touches me, nor do they turn to wave good-bye. Though I told them my story so they could understand, they leave with their faces blank, their good-byes as empty as my mother's soon-soon.

By the time the men who could have been my saviors leave, it is too late. I think my words over and hear their one unspoken thought: Guilty. The circle of lights arcs up when the car reverses and then is gone. The crunch of gravel under the tires fades quickly, and the melody of the night rises, a frog croaking there, a dog barking here, a squawk of a chicken awakened from its rest, a donkey braying. And couched between these sounds, silence.

What should I have told them instead? Should I have given a step-by-step account of what happened at the Rio Minho on Thursday? Or should I have told them of the times I saved my son from little dangers—a barking dog running too close, a charging ram, the shiny scissors and knives he liked to watch glint in light? There was that time he climbed on Grams's dresser for the wig she wore and sometimes aired by hanging it on the corner of the glass. "Mama hair," he said. He always played with it when she put it on, fascinated with removable hair, so unlike his own.

Perhaps this is the story I should have told. It is one that everybody knows, a story that was told over and over in the years before the government built the bridge. Grams told me the story and warned me never to cross the river alone. The Rio Minho is a hungry river, she said. Or maybe she said angry. She told me to always drop something in the river whenever I crossed the bridge. A stone, a stick, a one-cent coin. Anything. Just give the river something.

I always had something to drop. And Timothy loved to do the same. He counted out stones, and he never tired of hearing the soft plop, watching the little ripple in the water. He always looked up at me and laughed when he dropped one in. That boy had a belly full of laughter.

The woman in the story had two daughters and owned a piece of land across the river. One daughter was kind, the other mean. They say nobody who's mean should cross the Rio Minho because the person could drown. The woman sent her two daughters—one was Nora, the other was nameless—to her property across the river to get some ackees.

"If you no gimme some o' the ackee, you not goin' pass," Rio Minho called out when the girls got there. "De river goin' come down an' wash you 'way." Its words became a song.

The kind sister dropped an ackee. Nora held on to hers.

"Gimme one ackee, Nora, gimme one," Rio Minho sang again. "De river goin' come down and wash you 'way."

But Nora wouldn't give up her ackees. She sucked her teeth, drowned out her sister's words with her laughter. Nora walked. The river seemed to rise. It reached her waist, and Rio Minho sang again. As Nora walked, the water rose. It reached her armpits. The river sang faster and louder.

145

"Gimme, gimme, gimme one, Nora. De river goin' wash you 'way."

Nora walked farther, and the river rose higher. It reached her neck and swept Nora and the ackees away.

The Rio Minho is a hungry and angry river. Maybe all it asked was that I leave my son behind.

# The Wake

~

Nothing was as custom dictated it should be. The setup, the wake, which should have begun the first night of Timothy's death and continued every night till the burial, didn't begin until two days after Sonya arrived, five days late. Maisey came first, appearing in the dark, the flame of her kerosene lamp flickering in the breeze. She brought food, a pot of rice that she placed in front of her when she sat down on the verandah with Sonya and settled herself as if she were in her rightful place.

Other women followed. Pam, Carol, Mauva, Aunt Pearl, Lynette, Miss Doll. . . . They came one by one, each with some kind of food—fried plantains, curried goat, stewed chicken, pea soup, white rice, jugs of orange and carrot juice. There wasn't too much, just enough, as if they had planned what each woman would bring. There were forty, maybe fifty women. Ones who had witnessed the drowning. Still others who relived a prior experience of death. Others simply disgusted by a mother's apparent lapse. All, especially the younger women, driven by a desire to see justice upheld.

It shouldn't have been that way, especially since Sonya had just come from America and would have brought food. And she had. The family of the dead should have prepared the meal. And if any of the women wanted to help, they would have brought their husbands earlier to kill and skin the goat, to catch and kill the chickens. The women would have stayed to cut up and season the meat, steam the rice, fry or boil plantains, boil yams and sweet potatoes, cut up and grate the coconuts. If they wanted, they would have asked what they could bring. Instead, they brought food as if they had planned a picnic to which each woman would bring a portion of the meal.

Since the mourners had stayed away for four days, had refused to set foot in Grams's yard to mourn the death with Kelithe, neither Grams nor Kelithe anticipated the setup and didn't start the fire to prepare anything at all. Perhaps it wouldn't have been necessary for them to prepare any food either, since the women all came prepared and probably wouldn't have eaten what they cooked. But the mourners used Sonya's paper plates, plastic forks, and plastic cups.

The women should have distrusted Sonya—the outsider—but they didn't. They should have made her feel as guilty as they wanted Kelithe to feel, since Sonya was the foreigner facilitating Kelithe's departure. But they didn't. Fifteen years Sonya had been gone, but the years didn't matter. It seemed as if she had never left. Some of the women felt as if they were girls together again, gathering for some celebration, or playing together after their mothers had spent time washing at the river. For the older women, Sonya was just another daughter, a girl they had watched over when her mother wasn't present, as if she wasn't Kelithe's mother at all but someone to whom they believed an injustice had been done. They felt Kelithe had betrayed Sonya by her unmotherly act.

Their coming was also an apology for the stones thrown at her car, the broken windshield, her fright. Now the women viewed Sonya as a victim, as innocent, because someone had seen her leaving the police station. Not happy, not sad, but dissatisfied, the emptiness of not knowing weighting her head like a heavy basket. They came to fill the absence created by the not knowing.

Mostly, the women viewed Sonya as the one person who could ultimately prevent Kelithe from escaping unpunished. Sonya held Kelithe's papers, the plane ticket, the money. So the women courted Sonya, made her feel welcome, elevated her to a position that would otherwise have been held for an elderly woman who had earned the town's respect by being a mother to all.

Grams stayed away from the women.

Kelithe stayed away from the women and watched her mother hold court with Maisey at her side.

The women should have told stories, sung songs, danced, played ring games, told riddles intended to make the family forget the death, intended to cheer the grieving Sonya. But at first each woman who had been there at the river the day Timothy drowned reviewed the death, retold the story as she

149

remembered it. She—each woman—wanted to give Sonya the news she had gone in search of and hadn't found. Each woman stepped out of the dark shadows to stand before Sonya, and stood with her arms hanging and fingers intertwined in front of her the way a child would stand in front of a room full of strangers. Others stood with their hands hanging straight at their sides. However they stood, it was a pose of humility.

Each woman told of the splash she heard first, the soft scream. The boy's arms and head reaching above water. Running and grabbing the body and the attempts to revive the dying boy. Each woman said Kelithe had watched, must have known, must have seen, must have heard something. But didn't act. All because she wanted to leave.

Sonya listened, silent. She should have said, could have said, "Stop. Is my daughter you talkin' 'bout like that you know." But she didn't. She turned her head instead to each woman standing around her, nodded, and waited for her story to unfold. A woman wouldn't begin until Sonya had acknowledged that she was standing there.

Pam told her mother's story.

"Nine children, my mama have," Pam said. She didn't stand or twist her hands like the other women but sat at Sonya's feet and turned her head up as if she were waiting for a blessing. "Nine children. Six boys, three girls. Pure trouble Ronnie give 'er from the start. From the day 'e born. I know, I used to 'ave to watch 'im."

150    The women nodded. Pam turned her head to the women every now and then, looked at them for support she didn't seem to need. They knew her story as well as she did. But she sat as if she were on a stage, acting in a one-woman show.

"When school time come trouble. The teacher dem never want 'im dere. 'E wouldn't sit still. Wouldn't learn nothin'. All the beat Mama beat him nothin' can' stop the boy. But she stick by 'im. Is she born him. What else she can do?"

Again she looked up, took in the night, the women around.

"But is when 'e grow big, the real trouble start. 'E tek up with the weed. Sell little 'ere and dere. Smoke some. Something turn 'im. 'E a walk de streets now. But she don' turn 'er back. Is still 'er son. She cook and she carry food and go look for 'im. Anywhere 'e walk, she walk too. Anything he do, she do. 'Cause she mus' fin' her son and feed 'er son. No matter what people talk, she mus' fin' her son.

"Is only that I can think 'bout." Pam looked up at Sonya again, glanced toward the darkened house. "When I think of Timothy goin' down and the girl, Kelithe, standin' dere, not doin' nothin'. . . . What if my mother 'ad turn 'er back on Ron? Me? It 'urt me, ma'am, it 'urt me more than you can know to see the boy going down and the mother not doing nothing to 'elp."

It was as if each woman brought her painful past, as if by telling her story she was being healed. And it shouldn't have been that way at all. Sonya should have been on the receiving end of the healing. She should have been listening to songs, or games, or stories. Or listening to men drinking and talking and slapping dominoes on tables. Or running back and forth from the kitchen to the front of the house to make sure her guests were fed, not thirsty.

When Pam finished, when she received her blessing from Sonya, she receded into the shadows, and Beatrice stepped forward. She held her chin down, her eyes turned upward to

151

Sonya, and waited for the nod. The events of the night were like a play on a stage, scenes changing, a camera roving, the spotlight shifting. The women were a part of the night, barely moving except for small nods of their heads as each told her story. The bottle lamps they held, too, flickered like fireflies and didn't seem to be using much kerosene oil at all. None of the lamps flickered out. None of the women asked to borrow a little oil.

Beatrice placed her bottle lamp on the ground at her feet. The wavering light shone on her face, sometimes illuminating her eyes, sometimes showing only her moving lips. Her face shone as if it had been painted or oiled. She had wrapped her head in a glorious red kerchief and wasn't dressed like the others in the colors for mourning—purple, black, white. The points of her head kerchief stood up like antennas, were elongated like horns on her shadow.

Beatrice talked about her own daughter, who had died when she was eight of gastroenteritis.

"I boil tea, bissy, cerasee, arrowroot. She drink, but she run same way. Nothing I do make it stop. Everything Miss Maisey say, I follow. Nothin' work." Beatrice held her head up when she talked. She turned every now and then to face the women behind and draw encouragement from their constantly nodding heads.

"Shelly just get weaker and weaker. She used to like sew. All the needle she couldn't hol' no more. The little needle just slip out her hand. I tek her to the clinic. All day I wait. She wasn't bleedin', so they tell me I mus' wait, and I wait all day with her. Boil the water I give her, they say. Then sen' me home and say come back early morning if it don't stop. No doctor. Emergency at the hospital, and he gone already. The nurse say nothin' she can do. Come back morning time if things worse. All night I sit up with her. More tea, I give her.

"Maisey come and pray over her. 'Show me, Lord,' she say. 'Show me the way.' I kneel with her and pray. Shelly cry little and she moan. And I think, yes, she praying too. We wait. Give her more tea. I shut my eye for a little bit. Morning come. But morning too late."

Beatrice stopped, cleared her throat, and looked at the women with sad eyes. They knew her story, but she wanted them to feel again her three-year-old pain. She dabbed the corners of her eyes with her knuckles, folded and unfolded her hands, and waited. None of the women moved or cried but waited with her while she regained her strength. Sonya, too, watched and waited.

"Every day God bring, I ask myself what else I could do. What I do wrong. The pain never leave my heart." Beatrice held her hands over her left breast, looked around at the crowd. She turned one last time to Sonya, looked on her with tears glistening in the candlelight. "I know what you feeling. Imagine how I feel when I see the boy going down. The mother standing still . . . one more baby gone. A life gone before it even begin."

Sonya held out her hand, touched Beatrice's extended palm. Beatrice seemed to be drawing strength from the grasp, the gentle touch of Sonya's fingers. But Beatrice slid to the ground, weeping. Sonya stood, patted her back. Maisey reached for a cup, poured some water. Sonya held the cup to Beatrice's lips and with her skirt wiped the excess water that dribbled down Beatrice's chin. It was like mother and daughter, a baby dependent on and drawing from her mother's love.

Sonya should have been the child, the one taking strength. Instead, Sonya took the women's grief and made it her own. She imagined Timothy's last moments and added her own details to the stories the women told. She saw his mouth open wide for air but collecting water instead. His fingers reaching out and grasping a leaf, a handful of water. She imagined and held the stories, even though she couldn't recall his facial features. She had looked at the pictures around the house, she had seen the slight resemblance to Kelithe. But when she closed her eyes and thought of Timothy, what she saw was Kelithe as a little girl, her small eyes and thin eyebrows, high cheekbones and high forehead.

She thought of the boy struggling in the water, but didn't think of Kelithe as the women said she had stood. It was easier to think of the helpless boy than to imagine her daughter standing and not moving to grab him from the water.

It was easier for Sonya to think of the life lost than to imagine that she could have performed an act as final as the one the women described. She remembered how desperately she wanted to leave Standfast, how constricted she felt when her baby was first born, her one attempt to abort the baby. But even though Sonya thought of her own situation, imagined Kelithe desperately seeking an end to the monotony of life in Standfast, the finality of the act disturbed her. Even though Sonya had tried to abort her baby, she knew she would never have killed her five-year-old child had Grams decided against keeping the child.

Premeditated murder, Sonya thought, borrowing a word from detective shows. She stressed the word in her mind, used it to seal her position regarding the death of her grandson and Kelithe's role.

"A hear the pastor over at the Pentecostal church call a revival, a series o' prayer meetings for this week," Maisey said. "Yes, ma'am. Sunday gone he preach for de los' souls in Stand-fas'. All de ones who gone a foreign and de others who a rush to get them papers. A hear he call Kelithe name and pray fi God fi forgive her. Tha's what me hear." She tacked on her final statement, shielding herself, even though she didn't seem to need to. Many of the women around her had been there listening to the sermon.

"Yeah, so I hear too," Sonya said.

"Yes, ma'am. De pastor say only prayer can save Standfast now. We have to tek responsibility. He say in the service Sunday that the senseless death of Timothy is the reason he calling this meeting. When we as a people pray together, it can change things. Hmm-hmm. Yes, ma'am."

"So when the meetings begin?"

"Tuesday. Every day till Saturday. Till the funeral."

"Oh."

The woman ate then. It was nearly midnight. They'd been talking since nightfall. Somebody sang, a sad wailing cry. Sonya didn't eat but watched over the women as if they were still drawing strength from her, as if anything could happen if she took her eyes away for a brief moment.

In the candlelight, Sonya looked older, mature, almost regal. She had wrapped her hair earlier in preparation for bed. In the candlelight the points of her head-tie looked like a crown. Her satin housedress glistened in the dark. It was as if she and Maisey had switched roles, as if she had become the town mother, the town midwife, the old woman with stored knowledge of bush teas, the healer. Next to her Maisey seemed powerless, just old. Candles flickered on either side of Sonya, and the metal arms of the chair in which she sat looked bronze. Behind her the house was dark. Although the women glanced toward the house when they told their stories, when they described Kelithe's failure, Sonya never once glanced back.

When the plates were clean, they thanked Sonya as if she had prepared the meal.

"Tell me about Timothy," she asked in return. "Tell me what my grandson was like—"

For my son everything was a song: the wind in the trees, the *cleep-cleep* my mouth makes when I chew cane, the *crick-crack* of fire catching, the *pop* of chicken in hot oil, the *squish-squish* sound water and soap and cloth makes, Grams's slippers dragging on the floor. He walked behind her, his mouth making the *schleep-schleep* noise her slippers made, a laugh ready if she stopped and said, "Who there?"

"Schleep-schleep," he said. And it was always a joke.

He laughed an adult bellyful laugh, one hand akimbo, the other over his mouth, as if he had learned already that sometimes he had to keep his joy inside. I loved it when he laughed. It was like his whole body was laughing, like the sounds were coming from every part of his body, his toes, his knees, his elbow sticking out. It was the same when he cried. I never knew where on his body to touch him when I tried to comfort him. He pulled his arm away if I touched it and leaned forward if I rubbed his back. When he cried, it was as if the pain was not only on the inside but as if he hurt all over. But most of the time he was happy and singing.

"Sing, Mommy, sing," he used to say.

When the radio wasn't on, he pointed to it and said the same: "Sing, Mommy, sing." He used to stand in front of the radio, and when the songs were finished, he would sing, the words almost right, the tune perfect. He held a song in his mind all day. Sometimes he taught me the words.

At night we knelt side by side, and he sang his prayers: *Now I lay me down to sleep / I pray the Lord my soul to keep / If I should die before I wake / I pray the Lord my soul to take.* It was his song, his tune. And his voice was beautiful.

Grams would sing with him at night when she said her prayers and read and sang the Psalms. So he thought everything from a book was a song. He didn't want stories told. He wanted a song. The Jack and the Beanstalk song. The Anancy song. The Bible song.

"But that's not a song," I would say.

"Tell me Anancy song," he said, as if he knew a secret I didn't. Everything, anything was a song.

He sang the Twenty-third Psalm because it's Grams's favorite. He knew all the words. "The Lord is my shepherd," he used to sing in a tiny, breaking voice. He was beautiful. "I shall not want. He maketh me to lie down in green pastures. . . ."

"What is pastures?"

"Fields." And he picked up where he left off, as if nothing in the world mattered but his song.

Now when I walk through the house, I see his brown eyes following me, hear his songs in the walls. I can feel his fingers hanging on to just my little finger, his spit spraying in my face when he thought he tickled me and laughed. His hands, sticky from melting candy or powdered cheese from cheese doodles, clinging to my shirt, my breasts, my arms, when he didn't want to walk or stand on his own. I can hear his child's voice calling, "Mommy."

Now, I dream again a dream I used to have when I went away to school and when I used to think of the day my mother left me. Sweat drips, flows down the groove between my breasts, sticking to my thin cotton nightgown.

I am away at school again, Westwood. I am washing my hands in the bathroom. I am running my hands under the water, much longer than I know I should, because for the first time in a long time our principal and house mothers have stopped reminding us that the tanks are almost empty. I stare too long at my large eyes, my thick hair, parted down the middle, the two braids running along my hairline near my ears and disappearing in the back. I think how my hair would look straightened, large curls flowing and falling. Pretty.

I look out the bathroom door, down the graded hill where we stand for prayers every morning. It is empty, all around, not a blue-and-white uniform in sight. The sun burns down on the dusty ground, almost white.

I run to all the classrooms, the chemistry labs, through the staff room where no students are allowed, down the stairs to the dorms. No one. I am trying hard not to cry because I know there is no one around to hear me. I run toward the principal's office, up the stairs, past the library. I am nearing the top of the steps when I see the ladder and the gray hair that sets the principal's body apart from the rest of the girls. Up in the clouds they go . . . up, up, and away.

The dream always ends there, or maybe that's all that I choose to remember. But I don't tell Grams about this dream. I dream that dream almost every night now, even though my mother and I are together for the first time in many years and I used to dream that dream when I thought of her being gone. I dream it now when I think of Timothy, because when I think of my son, I think of my mother.

I loved my son. Only once I thought about leaving him. I tried to get a job in Kingston, pick up a dream I'd buried. The dream where I would be a journalist, reading the evening news and standing in front of the prime minister, asking him what he was doing to our country. At school I practiced reading, pronouncing words over and over, accented like my mother. Perfect English. I joined the debating club, read the scripture lessons from the Bible at worship as often as I could, spoke up, always spoke out. When Timothy came, I forgot the dream, buried it in motherhood.

When Timothy turned two, I went to Kingston for a job, told Grams to keep him inside so he wouldn't watch me leave, wouldn't think long about my fingers waving good-bye or a back that wouldn't turn around to stop his tears from falling.

Nobody wanted a girl who hadn't finished high school. No matter how I spoke or read, or how quickly my fingers flew across the typewriter keys. All that was left was keeping shop, ringing up groceries.

The rattle of the coins and sound of the machine sounded like Timothy's songs. I kept making those sounds over and over in my mind, wondering how I could get my son to sing the same songs too. I wondered how my mother had done it, how she'd replaced my voice, forgot to kiss me good-bye.

The first morning when Timothy woke and didn't see me there, he stopped singing. And I knew that I was the reason for his songs.

"See what happen when you leave you' chile?" Grams said. "He forget you."

I wasn't making enough to bring him with me there. I couldn't think of my son not singing because I didn't tell him good-bye. I didn't want him to think of his mother as always going away.

I came back to Standfast, and the happiness spread across Grams's face. "He's your responsibility," she said.

Soon-soon, my mother had said. Just wait a little.

So I came back to Standfast and stayed with my baby, nursed him. Planted peas and corn with Grams and sold what we didn't use. I was there with him in the clinic when he pushed the pencil eraser in his ear, there when the doctor poured that oily liquid into his ear and gently eased the eraser out.

My son didn't like water. And that liquid in his ear made him squirm and kick his feet. He kicked the table, and the bottles and needles rattled. He cried some more because the things had frightened him and he saw the tweezers in the doctor's hands when the doctor reached out to settle the table.

Timothy loved the sound of water, but he didn't like water. He watched the falling rain, but he didn't play in the mud because there was always water afterward. Cold water. Even when I left a basin of water out in the sun all day so it would be warm at nighttime for his bath, he still cried. He fought me as if there was something in the water I couldn't see. Sometimes all I could do was wipe his body down with soap and forget the basin of water.

160

"Water." He pointed as if it was a bad thing.

Once I put a basin of water in the sun so he could play with his shadow and learn to like water. "Timothy," he said when he looked at his shadow. "Timothy in water." He shook his head no and turned away.

I was there, always, for my son. No matter what these women say. I was there. I wouldn't leave him behind. I came back from Kingston and waited for my mother. I'm still waiting for my mother. I'm waiting for her to say, "Kelithe wouldn't." To look toward the house and see me standing here listening to what the women say. But the stories go on and on all night.

After midnight the men arrived. Teacher Williams led the group. They brought the songs, the riddles, the games, beer, rum, the cheer for the women. They sat around Sonya in groups and paid her their respects. She received their condolences like a grieving mother because she had the women's stories to make her own. The men, too, told Sonya what Timothy was like, the good things about a young life cut off too early.

Sonya stepped fully into the role that should have been Kelithe's. Teacher Williams held Sonya as she cried. Maisey remained at Sonya's right side and wiped her tears. She cried for a while, not loudly. She didn't bawl, but her chest heaved and her body trembled. The women sat silently and waited for Sonya to cry her first batch of tears. It was as if the women knew that Sonya couldn't mourn until she had heard their stories. She cried for the grandson she didn't know, the young life lost. And not for her daughter, labeled by the women, by Standfast, as a murderer.

161

"Read me the Thirty-first Psalm." Sonya held up her head a little. She knew instinctively what was expected of her in such a situation despite her fifteen-year absence.

"In thee, O Lord, do I put my trust; let me never be ashamed; deliver me in thy righteousness," Teacher Williams read, a steady baritone.

Maisey held Sonya's hands while he read. Sonya wiped her eyes and wept.

"Rock of Ages," one of the women called from the shadows when Teacher Williams finished the Psalm. The group sang, followed it up with "Jesus Lover of My Soul," "At Evening When the Sun Is Set." Teacher Williams then read the Ninety-first Psalm.

The songs continued. Sonya wept, didn't once look toward the house.

There was no lull. The songs came one right after another, with Bible passages in between. Somebody called out the first line of a song, started singing, and the group picked it up.

"All right," Maisey said. "Time now for something different."

"Riddle me this, riddle me that. Guess me this riddle, and perhaps not," Teacher Williams said. The men and women settled in for a long night of games and songs.

Ask me and I will tell . . .

. . . the dream last Wednesday of the faceless blue dress rowing a boat on the still river, away to the endless sea. No boundaries. No anchor. No baby weighing the blue dress down.

. . . the long-ago dream of all the girls at school climbing the ladder to heaven. All but me.

. . . of the endless nights when Grams told me stories to take over the places in my mind where my mother stayed.

There was one about the River Mumma, the mother of the river. She had a golden comb and all the riches of the river to give to whomever she wanted. I was the one she chose. She was my mother. I was her daughter, a river woman with a purpose.

. . . of the endless nights immediately after my mother left when I stayed awake, asking Grams over and over how come there was a place in the sky where people lived, even though they were not dead, not gone to heaven. She said the plane was like a kite; it went up, floated with the wind, and came back down, but in a different place.

. . . about the lie a deaconess told me once when she said that my mother left me behind because men steal little children there. "You wouldn't want to go there," she said, and described a dark place, not a place filled with cloudlike snow. Her eyebrows met when she wrinkled her face, and I thought of her widow's peak crawling down to meet her eyebrows, too.

. . . of the times I went back to school with too few panties and worn-down shoes because my mother had forgotten to send the new things in time for the new term.

. . . of the night I discovered *soon* turned backwards is *noos*. Noos(e). No os. No us. I couldn't tell Timothy "Soon."

. . . of the night before my baby drowned. Of the words whispered to the wind and Miss Maisey. "From I turn sixteen I raising children and still can' get no rest. First mine, then Kelithe. Now the baby, too?"

"You too ol' for that now," Miss Maisey said.

"Sonya want her leave the baby first. Get settled and bring him up later."

At first the wind carried the words. And then I drew nearer.

163

"But you see how long Sonya's *later* last. How long now she gone?" Miss Maisey knew, but she asked anyway.

"Fifteen years now. I too ol' to keep a baby boy."

And Maisey carried those words and made it her story when my baby drowned. It's almost as if I can hear her scratchy voice whispering the words behind her hand to anyone who will listen. "She couldn't find anybody to keep the baby, so she watched him drown."

Ask me, and I will tell the words Maisey didn't hear the morning after.

"Six months," Grams said. "I give you six months to settle and take the boy. Don't do like you' mother and leave you' chile for somebody else to raise. He's you' own responsibility."

I told her thanks, but kept my back turned because Timothy was sitting on the floor singing a song, and I remembered the time before when I left and he had stopped singing. And I remembered, too, my mother's back, the way her hair brushed her exposed neck, her dark fingers smoothing down the front of her dress and brushing my body's imprint away.

Later that morning Miss Maisey came. Timothy was holding my skirt, hiding his face and peeking from one eye.

"Boy, show you' face," Miss Maisey said. "What you goin' do when you' mother gone leave you?"

Timothy stepped back, and I felt the emptiness where he had held my leg. He looked up with sad eyes, a reconstructed face, as if he remembered the time before when I had left and he stopped singing. He went to Grams and held her skirt instead.

I looked down on Timothy and knew I couldn't plan on leaving him behind.

I sang for him, and he came back to me. We left for the river, he walking behind me and singing an old folk song that Grams taught him:

> *Hol' him, Joe! Hol' hi, Joe!*
> *Hol' him, Joe, and no let him go.*
> *Hol' him, Joe, Hol' him, Joe,*
> *Hol' him, Joe, and no let him go.*
> *Donkey wan' water,*
> *Hold him Joe.*
> *Donkey too frisky,*
> *Hol' him, Joe . . .*

That's the last song my son ever sang.

Ask me and I will tell of the dreams I gave Timothy after my mother said, "You have to leave the baby for now," and after Miss Maisey reshaped his face with her uncalled-for words.

I gave him images of what we would do when we got there. First, I would give him a radio to play his own songs. And a television so he could watch the singers dance. And I would get a video camera to take pictures of him singing and dancing, and we'd watch the videos together and laugh. Just me and him. But not till we got there. I told him what I remembered reading about Coney Island, tried to draw a picture in the sky of the big blue Wonder Wheel. We would ride the train, and he asked what that was.

"It looks like twenty big buses joined together," I told him.

"We goin' on a bus train?"

"A train."

"To where?"

165

"Alexandria. Coney Island. New Jersey." The names or places wouldn't matter to him. I made some up.

Ask me, and I will tell. That morning Timothy was happy. I had a plan, and he was in it. He believed me when I said the story wasn't the way Miss Maisey told it.

"Why Miss May say you was leavin' me?"

I'd hoped he had forgotten.

"Nothing. She never had nothing better to say."

I couldn't tell him I wouldn't leave him for long because the one thing I remembered most was the way his face changed and the emptiness when he let go of my leg and held on to Grams instead.

"Hol' on to my shirt." I waited. "We riding the bus train over the Rio Minho."

He laughed.

Dream about that, I told him on our way to the river. Dream, my son, dream.

# Sonya's People

~

All day people come and fill the house with whispers and grunts, their talk of good times and bad, arthritic hands and knees, bad hearts, so and so who's not doing well, or so and so who came back from foreign to live in the big house he built out in Orange Valley. Those are the things they talk out loud when I am near or when Grams sits with them. At other times they sound like boarding-school girls after lights-out, wanting to talk and having to avoid being heard by an ever-watchful house mother. Always talk about me. At school then; in my own house now.

They talk to my mother and sometimes Grams. Never to me.

Miss Maisey is always here. I'm not sure if she left since she got here last night. I listen to her gossip, to her telling my mother things as if they have been best friends for years and watch my mother slap her shoulder and laugh. Grams doesn't laugh. She sits with them but she doesn't laugh.

When the house is empty, my mother listens to the call-in radio shows. The radio plays all day long, even though the breakfast sounds, the pots, metal banging against metal, and the fork beating against the dish as she gets ready to scramble her eggs, drowns out the British voice that reads the eight o'clock *BBC World News*. But she listens anyway, sitting with her plate of food next to the radio, listening to the early callers who have problems in their love lives, the ones who think a doctor on the radio can solve their medical problems. She listens till late morning when the political problems come, when everyone tries to solve, or bring to light, all of Jamaica's problems.

One person talks briefly about a situation in Standfast, the accidental drowning of a boy that the police refuse to investigate. JoAnna. It sounds like JoAnna. We call her Jonah because her mouth is as big as a whale. She swallows stories whole and spits them back out without any care for the people inside the stories. I know she's the one who took my story on the radio. She says that Standfast deserves to be known. Every so often she takes her mother's money and runs off to Kingston, to Halfway Tree Road, to the Gleaner Company, and tells anyone who will listen what her story is. Sometimes she runs to the nearest pay phone and calls the radio shows. And I know it's her this time. Nobody else.

Jonah talks about the roadblock and how hard it is to sell anything, the roundabout route that buses and trucks have to take because of the fires that continue burning. She says the town has come to a standstill, and something must be done before all hell breaks loose.

But Standfast has always been at a standstill. Nobody here does anything. No nationwide riot has touched this place.

My mother listens, but she doesn't comment about anything at all.

There was a time when we used to listen to the radio together, when I was three or four, the earliest memories I have of her. She listened every evening to a story, "Dulcie," about a duppy—a ghost. There was a haunting voice I remember, and even though I was too young to understand the fear of the dead walking, I was scared sometimes at night when the candles were blown out by the breeze. I was too young then to understand what it was about. But I would sit with her and Grams, very quietly, and when the story was done I would laugh when they laughed, waiting till the next day for the continuation of the story. But that was long ago, long before I understood much of anything.

She is quiet now, keeping her thoughts to herself, not even commenting on the news stories that shock everyone else. She says nothing about the gunman who burst into a house somewhere in Kingston and killed a sleeping family of four. She says nothing about the prisoners who escaped and have been terrorizing a small village up in the hills of St. Mary. Nothing at all. Grams sits with her, but I'm not sure she listens. She doesn't comment either. But even when we are alone, Grams doesn't usually comment on the news, and I'm not surprised by her quietness. She used to say that she hears of too much evil in the world and doesn't have to listen to the radio to know more of it.

169

"Hearing that a gunman break into a shop and kill the owner for a little hundred dollars not going do anything to me but make me thank God it wasn't me. And that kind of prayer too selfish. So why bother? Why listen, eh?"

That's a conversation Grams and I had often. But she doesn't say the same when her neighbors come by with news, good or bad. She listens and sometimes passes the news on to me.

Now I wait for my mother's love. For years I waited for my mother's hand brushing my eyes closed. Her good-night touch. Her fingers parting and plaiting my hair. A dress ironed with her love. A mother who sat with my teachers at school and said, "Yes. She work real hard all the time." Hers and Grams's voices singing the A, B, C and 1, 2, 3 songs. But it was always only Grams's voice. Only Grams's voice at Basics School graduation and her lips smiling when I walked off the stage with the other children.

I waited for my mother's lipstick kiss at the airport that one time, but she turned away from me and went behind the blue glass. She kept her kiss and brushed her dress down instead.

I want my mother to ask me what she asked the women last night.

# Standfast's Awakening

~

It may have been the hundreds of unfulfilled government promises or the absence of promises that should have been made but weren't even considered.

Maybe the spirit of a former warrior—incensed by what had happened, infuriated that the death of an innocent child had failed to generate much interest, furious about the continuing insignificance of Standfast—awakened from a hundred-year sleep and prodded awake Standfast's young adults.

The way some people told it, the demonstration in Standfast shifted because Pam took the time to walk to the bus stop at the edge of town to go to the out-of-town police station and tell the uniformed officer, who looked down on her thin T-shirt, that a crime had been committed. A little boy had walked into the water, and she was sure the mother had watched but done nothing to help.

"She was right dere, sir. Right dere, I tell you."

He raised his eyes from her breasts, from the lacy bra under the thin shirt, to ask her where the crime had taken place.

"Standfast," she said. "Rio Minho."

He smiled when she answered, dropped his eyes again, and waited for the description of the crime to unfold.

"Things have always been quiet out that way," he said. "Twenty years now I on the force. Never been out there. What going on out there now?"

He took no notes as she talked, but his eyes took note, moving up, down, and across her body. When she finished, she felt the need to gather herself close, and she crossed and uncrossed her legs and rubbed her ankles together. She looked down at the red mud caked to her shoes, up at the officer looking down at her legs, gathered herself together, and left.

"Miss? Miss?" he called out as she left.

But she didn't look back. She heard his hmm-hmm, the smack of his lips, and walked faster. She didn't stop walking, didn't wait for a bus to drop her near Standfast. She walked all the way home, oblivious of the buses that zipped near her body, the rush of air from the moving vehicles that rustled the plastic bag in her hand, the tail of the kerchief on her head.

Pam was angry that the police officer didn't take notes, didn't take her story seriously, didn't take his eyes from her body long enough to concentrate on the pain in her eyes. She was bothered that he didn't promise to send an officer over to investigate what she considered an unforgivable crime. What mattered in Standfast didn't matter to anyone outside the town, and she vowed to change that.

Or it may have been that once again no one took JoAnna's story seriously. Nobody called in to the radio programs to talk about the seriousness of the crime in Standfast. No reporter from the *Daily Gleaner* or JBC or RJR came to take her story, to listen to a firsthand account of the tragedy or write an editorial about corrupt police officers. Nobody cared about a crime in Standfast, an out-of-the-way town not found on any maps.

While Standfast's stories—Timothy's drowning, limited medical opportunities, below-average sanitary conditions, no nearby school—received no notice, police probed the ashes, the half-burned offices of the Orange Valley Agriculture Marketing Cooperative for clues to the whereabouts of Sam Shepherd, the director of the cooperative, and millions of missing dollars. Police ransacked Shepherd's newly constructed five-bedroom house and allowed photographers to capture images of the house's carpeted interior, four television sets lined up beside a computer and a microwave, leather couch, and two safes built into the concrete wall. The safes, the police pointed out, were the most damaging evidence of Shepherd's guilt.

Politicians descended on Orange Valley, offering advice to residents whose money was tied up in the cooperative, and promised to return every hundred and every thousand of dollars.

"Jus' yesterday I was due to get my share back, and Shepherd say come back today 'cause the money no ready yet," a bawling woman told reporters. "Five thousand dollars and more I lose, and the children to go a school. Where the money to come from now?"

According to the newspaper reports, MP Jose Beckford reached into his pocket and pulled out five one-hundred-dollar bills. He pledged then to get the rest of the woman's money and all monies owed to everyone else. He smiled wide in the accompanying photograph. One arm was draped around the mother, the other around her youngest child.

Standfast's residents read the stories of Orange Valley's plight in the daily newspaper, eyed the photographs of the politicians standing proudly in front of and beside Orange Valley's residents. Orange Valley didn't have to protest to get police attention, to draw government representatives. The desired response was automatic.

The boy's ignored drowning, the possibility that Kelithe would escape accountability, the fact that Orange Valley got immediate response and Standfast didn't, marked the final insults that combined to ignite the sleeping spirits of Standfast. Individually, they weighed the things that had kept Standfast from demanding attention. The forgotten promise of the bridge. The younger people—those nearing thirty and for whom the story of the ignored promise was only a folktale—set ablaze the wooden, rickety, single-car bridge that spanned Rio Minho. This time the women didn't search their yards for neglected or rotting things. They didn't ask the men for help. Later, men would say they smelled kerosene when they arrived. The women would neither admit nor deny they deliberately poured kerosene on the rotting wooden slats. But they watched the fire blaze out of control.

The young people burned the old bridge that had caused their grandparents so much contention, that reminded the old of a long-ago, abandoned promise. The old wooden bridge that swayed in the breeze and rattled when cars or two-ton trucks drove over it. The same bridge that politicians had promised year after year to replace with a modern metallic structure, with sturdy metal posts embedded deep in the river's soft dirt, and wide enough so two cars could pass simultaneously.

The blasted bridge. The old men never forgot the hours they put in building what should have been the symbol of Standfast's future. Some called Rio Minho's glistening stones Standfast's gold, and dreamed of a day when somebody else would come back to set right what the government had long ago set wrong. When they came, they, too, watched the burning and accepted the fire as an inevitable thing.

Teacher Williams called the bridge Standfast's pride, the one thing besides the ancestors' glorious fight that truly was the town's. When he taught, he stressed the way the men came together to build the bridge to mark the town. He underlined the way the women and children stepped forward to fulfill their roles. They planted and fed the working men. After the men finished, everyone celebrated—for days. Standfast was moving forward. But nobody said, "Finally." The young ones were too polite, didn't want to upset the old folks. The old folks kept quiet, not wanting to bring attention to their failure. The women thought about those early lessons from the man everyone calls Teacher. They were happy to be the ones responsible for the undoing of Standfast's pride.

Teacher Williams's wife called it a jilted bride who refused to step away from the altar and find a way to hide her empty hands. When she took her place among the neighbors watching the vibrant fire, she mouthed, "Finally," and imagined a metallic structure, like ones she had seen spanning other rivers, in its place.

The Marshall granddaughters knew their grandfather had first established his bakery shop at the foot of the bridge to sell bottled drinks, beef patties, meat loaf, Red Stripe beer, spiced buns, and cheese to the men who would come to labor there. Nothing was ever baked at the shop. Instead the shop held everything—dry goods, canned foods, vegetables, flour filled with weevils, rice with weevils, brown sugar with too many lumps, molasses, Milo, Ovaltine, shoe polish, bleach. Nobody called it Bridge Bakery, although that's what the hand-painted sign had said for nearly sixty years. "Go down to Mister Marshall and get me . . . ," was what mothers said. The grandchildren didn't dream, as their grandfather had that day, that one day someone would establish a business mining riverbed stones and provide the opportunity for his family business to earn the Bridge Bakery name.

Sixty years. It took Standfast sixty years to let go of a promise and move forward.

Orange flames shot up in the black night, hanging suspended, before the bridge's wooden slats fell to the dark water below. Soft splashes. A clap against rocks. Red, orange flames suspended from one end of the solid earth swayed above the rushing water, cavernous blackness beside it. Invisible smoke spiraled, clouding, covering the small houses and filling their tiny rooms.

176    The young women shattered the symbol that had kept the elder folks mired in the past and waiting for their government to hand out a future. The young women took charge. Standfast's not-so-successful demonstration—started first because

the women were incensed by a mother's callous act, second because outsiders placed no value on Timothy's lost life, and third because each slight culminated in one unbearable insult—changed shape. It was as if the early ancestors, cheated of their one chance to defend the town, entered into the women in one final attempt to reclaim some dignity for Standfast.

# The Bridge's Fate

The offending air woke Sonya. She jumped up with one hand at her throat, the other at her nose blocking the smell, choking, and gasping. When she opened her eyes, what she saw first was not her daughter standing over her but the image of a john crow with its wings spread wide, the figure similar to the one in her dream. Sonya sat up and held her hands the way she would have held them to cradle a five-year-old—the young child in the dream frightened by the black john crow. Her eyes were on Kelithe, but what she saw was her little girl in plaits, crying the way she cried in the dream.

*"Mummy, Mummy, look!"*

*"Not now. When I finish this."*

*"But, Mummy, look. Look dere!"*

*"Not now, Kel. A have to finish cook before night come. Go back outside and play."*

*"'Fraid to go outside." She wraps her hand in my skirt. A little tug, and my plaid skirt, already loose because the elastic in the waist is old and stretched, starts sliding down, over my belly.*

*"You pulling my skirt down, girl." I pull up the skirt quickly to cover the line of curly black hair that runs up the middle of my stomach. "Wha' out dere for you to 'fraid of? It's the same yard you play in all the time." I push her with my hips, just a little, away from the hot pots on the coal stove. She stumbles but doesn't let go.*

Sonya's hand mirrored the actions in the dream. She slid her hand over her belly and pulled at the loose nightclothes, as if she were pulling the dream skirt back in place. She moved her hands away from her body in a shoving motion, but didn't move her eyes from Kelithe's face.

"Ma'am?"

She didn't hear her adult daughter calling her in the way she would call a stranger, but heard instead the crying of her young daughter.

*"Crows. Big black john crows outside. One o' dem chase me."*

*She is still pulling on my skirt, wrapping her fingers in my clothes and pressing against my knees, begging me to believe. A hot teardrop falls on my foot, and I look up toward the window.*

*Black john crows are circling the house, out of place. There is nothing dead for vultures to eat. I stand behind the*

179

*thin blue curtain, staring through the glass windowpanes. Her fingers are clutching my shirt, digging into my skin. One of the crows is sitting on the stone wall, looking directly in the window.*

*"That one." Kelithe points a dirty finger at the bird. It moves off its perch, closer to the window, and tries to sit on the narrow ledge. Its beak smacks against the glass. The bird stumbles, its small back eyes never leaving my face. I think of the rotten bodies of cows, goats, stray dogs or cats, that its claws have torn apart, its beak has ripped to shreds. It tries again to sit on the ledge.*

*Kelithe screams and hides behind my legs, her plaits rubbing against my legs. I tell myself I must close the window, and I move quickly, dragging her weight along. The bird lunges at the window.*

"No! No!"

"Ma'am? You a'right?"

"What you mean?"

"Nothing. Grams say to come get you. Fire nearby."

She watched her daughter's back, stiff, shoulders high, and then the arching eyebrows and wrinkled forehead when Kelithe turned to look.

Sonya felt her heart. She knew she should have been thinking what her mother would have been thinking about the dream, that the vulture chasing her daughter meant something. Something would happen. And not something good. But she thought, instead, of her daughter as the vulture, standing over her body with wings spread wide and remembered the stories the women told. She remembered, too, the bird that had

180

come before, the morning after her arrival, and sat on the fence with its wings spread before her mother chased it away with a stone.

She wanted to but couldn't feel the protective urge of motherhood that sprang up for an instant in the dream and afterward when she rocked on the bed in front of her grown daughter like an old person whose mind had wandered off.

"Whatever happen now, she still you' daughter and you have to stan' by her." The long-ago voice of her mother. Words spoken when Kelithe had turned up pregnant and she buried her anger because she felt again the sting of her father's belt and sweat pouring onto broken skin and the pain of trying to abort the baby that her own father had failed to beat out of her.

Sonya heard her mother shuffling toward the room and moved then to grab the clothes she had worn during the day.

"Hurry up, hurry up. We don't know what going on. Maybe somebody need help."

To Sonya, it seemed that God had descended with his chariots of fire. He had come calling, rousing the sleeping women, keeping them from stifling in the fumes of the burning bridge. Some women wore green, yellow, and pink curlers in their hair. Thin, torn nightgowns half covered their bodies. They came running with sleepy children in their arms, some being dragged behind. Bare feet clapped against the solid earth and the jutting stones.

Men came running too, belatedly, half-empty beer bottles and machetes in their hands, ready to fight whatever battle needed fighting.

The dreamers were drawn to the bridge, mesmerized by

181

the fire, the conflagration. Someone had heeded God's call. A chorus began, and the dreamers turned the night into a revival meeting. Everyone swayed to the rhythm, accompanied the songs with their claps, foot stomps. Someone shook a bottle filled with stones, and others joined in, the ping and clatter of stone against glass ringing above the voices. Others filled empty aluminum soda cans with stones, adding to the noise, the praises. The lilting voices shattered the night's peace, woke up the dead, and set the dogs howling. They felt the spirits. The women, especially.

Sonya didn't think it was the religious spirits. She could only think the forgotten stories of war, the ancestors who had stood fast long ago, ready to fight to save the free town. It was their spirits, she knew, that had reinhabited Standfast.

The impromptu choir sounded like a mixture of a Pentecostal and a Baptist church at the height of a night revival meeting. Only there was no one preaching, no one calling the sinners to repent and be baptized, no one calling for the sick, the crippled, the blind, to come forward and be healed. No one calling names.

> *O my Lord, somebody's calling my name.*
> *O my Lord, somebody's calling my name.*
> *What shall I do?*

Everybody forgot that without the bridge they couldn't cross the river there but would have to walk two miles east or another few miles west to get to the other side of the river.

But that wouldn't be a problem for days. The roads remained empty during the daylight hours, the way they had been when Sonya first arrived. No one protested any wrong-doing. No one marched with banners. The shops were closed. Standfast market was for once empty. The mud brought into the market the prior Wednesday, with the ground produce and on the tires of trucks, was caked and crumbled, mixed in with dried banana leaves. The stalls were empty, cracks of sunlight streaming through the wooden slats and through the wire mesh, reflecting circles of sunlight against the dark interior. The smell of rotted fruit and animal waste still lingered.

And the smell would get stronger, filling the town with an even stronger stench, when the fruits and the vegetables no one had been able to sell in Standfast market or outside the town began to rot.

> *Jehovah Jireh, my provider, His grace is sufficient for me.*
> *Jehovah Jireh, my provider, His grace is sufficient for me.*
> *My Lord shall supply all my needs, all my needs*
> *According to his wishes in glory*
> *Glory, He gave his angels charge over me*
> *Jehovah Jireh cares for me, for me, for me*
> *Jehovah Jireh cares for me.*

"Look, look, de fire a spread."

The smell of the smoke rising up from the burning bridge changed to a rancid stench as the bushes and trees growing green along the banks of the river, next to the bridge, caught fire. The black faces were illuminated in the darkness, showing their fear that the fire could spread further to their little houses on the side of the river.

"Move back, Ma. Move back over there." Sonya ran with

183

the other women to grab pails and buckets. She didn't stop to look if her mother had moved or if Kelithe had come behind her as she ran back to the house. She felt a spirit inside her, quickening her pace, and a kinship with whoever had set the bridge ablaze. She sprinkled water around their house first, wetting the earth, the bushes, the coffee plants, the rows of croton and hibiscus trees, with a hope that the fire wouldn't spread too far too fast.

Even though the bridge was far enough away from the house, Sonya ran and watered, because without the rains anything could happen.

"Quick. Bring some buckets."

Men were shouting, moving with the women when Sonya returned.

"Unno get some water. Move back! Move back!"

All singing had subsided. Metal pails clashed against the rocks as the women and men set the pails down below standpipes. The sounds took over from the singing voices. The women, who should have been standing back with their children and watching their men beat the fire, were out there, too, cutting down bushes with their machetes, swinging buckets of water.

A boy started singing, "London Bridge is burning down . . ." "Hush up you mout'," the woman standing over him snapped.

"We need more water. Bring some more o' them buckets."

"Move faster! Wood burn quick you know!"

"Sprinkle some of de water round the houses over dere. An' keep the bushes wet so the fire don' spread any further." Mr. Thompson took over, directing the action. "Quick! Unno move faster! Step like unno have life."

184

Men slashed away at the bushes, the green growth around the banks of the river. The metal cutlasses hit against the rocks, the sharp sound rising into the night. Branches and leaves flew, the men's strength too much for the bushes. When another path was clear, another group of men formed a line, balancing precariously above the rushing river, to pass fresh water from the river to others above. Like a chain gang, they humphed as they passed full buckets of water above their heads, averting their faces to avoid the water splashing over the rims of the pails.

Sonya joined the men, swinging her pail, humphing as they humphed.

"If any o' you get tired, we have more people up here that can come down and help," someone shouted from up above the river.

"We almos' there. Couple more buckets," Mr. Johnson, still in control, shouted.

But the fire they thought they had under control rose again, enveloping Pearl's house. The wooden structure crackled under the fire, its sloping roof black against the orange flames.

"O God. Mi house. Lawd Jesus, mi house." Pearl, whom everybody called Aunt, jumped with renewed purpose, grabbing a bucket full of water from somebody's hand, throwing water against the flames. More people started running, and the chain of men and women leading from the rushing river started hauling the pails faster.

They humphed and humphed.

"One more bucket!"

Humph. Humph.

185

Pearl and her children watched the space where their house had been, shivering from the fear of being homeless. They stood huddled against one another; the youngest, Marie, sucked her thumb. The smoke, the color of the night, lingered in the air. There was no wind to blow it away.

Sonya watched Pearl, the others tired and wiping sweat from their faces. She looked around for Kelithe. She didn't see her daughter but saw her mother standing in the shadows of another house.

Even though Sonya had heard the women's stories, it was the defining action of a town used to inaction, the blackened steel of the bridge, that sealed her conviction that what they said about Kelithe was true.

# News Reports

⌒

## THE JAMAICAN STAR

### Standfast Residents Outraged
### Mother Free after Watching Son Drown

Standfast—Nov. 15—Standfast residents, outraged that a mother has been allowed to walk free following the drowning death of her son, last night blocked the main road from Orange Valley to Alexandria after burning the bridge spanning the Rio Minho.

The roadblock on the Orange Valley Road follows days of silent protests and roadblocks within Standfast.

Timothy Williams, three, drowned last Thursday at the Rio Minho here, while his mother, Kelithe Williams, 20, was washing clothes. Residents are upset that several attempts to get the police to investigate what they call a suspicious death have been rebuffed.

Women who were at the river last Thursday said Williams had left the boy asleep under a tree, while she washed. Eyewitnesses said the boy woke and was walking toward his mother when he accidentally fell into the river, not too far away from his mother's feet. The witnesses, however, were unable to accurately judge the boy's distance from the mother.

The three-year-old boy was retrieved by several of the other women. But he had already drowned.

Residents here say the death could have been averted. While the boy may have accidentally fallen into the water, eyewitnesses charge the boy was close enough to his mother to have drawn her attention to his flailing in the water or to his cries.

Police officials, however, declined to comment on the town's allegations that Williams watched her son drown. At least one police officer manning the station's front desk said he had not heard about the boy's drowning.

Residents also allege that Williams failed to rescue her drowning son because he had been the only obstacle to her departure to the United States. Williams had recently received word from her mother abroad that she had obtained the necessary papers for her departure from the island. The girl, who dropped out of high school at age 15, had been looking for a relative or friend to keep the child until she was able to support him fully in the states, residents said.

"She didn't have anywhere to leave him, so she watch him drown," said Miss Maisey, who preferred to identify herself as the town mother.

Outside of Standfast, people who rely on the Orange Valley Road are angry and demanding action from the government.

Police from Orange Valley are awaiting assistance from the Jamaica Defense Force to handle the growing demonstration. Police sources said that it appears that people are gathering from other towns to fan the demonstration because Standfast itself is a relatively small town with roughly 600 residents.

A spokesman for the station declined to comment. When asked why the police had no record of the incident, Orange Valley's mayor replied, "We have a small police force here. Not every incident receives the attention it deserves."

But Standfast's residents, who have long been outraged by the many service cuts the area has suffered and the lack of government concern about installing telephone lines, running electricity, or reopening the Standfast Health Clinic, are still not satisfied with the promise of an investigation. They charge that Alexandria and Orange Valley have been developed at the expense of Standfast.

Residents say the schools have also deteriorated under the present government, with less than half of the town's eligible sixth-grade students sitting the Common Entrance Exam and only a handful of those passing the examinations.

"It just goes to show you how little life here is worth, how little the government thinks of us," said Austin Weekes, pastor of the Standfast Tabernacle Church. "We have no hospital, no clinic, and the drivers refuse to pick up dead people. So that means we don't have an investigation into the death."

"The investigation should have happened long time," said Macie Hopkins, longtime resident. "She should have been behind bars a'ready."

It's the first thing I see. Next to Grams's Bible and my mother's bottles of perfume and makeup on the dresser.

Words like those bring Timothy back to me, again and again. Sometimes I feel him still kicking inside me, and at nights before I fall asleep, the heavy tenderness of milk-swollen breasts return. I think of his first moments alive, his head covered with thin, curly hair, his lips moving, sucking, searching for a nipple with milk.

I bend over in pain and cramps because of the memories of his birth. Hours and hours of labor, and no one to help me through the pain. No baby father to hold my hand or wipe my tears. No mother. Grams too old for a hospital room. She stays at home and prays for a healthy great-grandchild.

At night when I sleep, I imagine the doctor again looking at me, feeling for the natural widening, the baby's head, recommending a C-section. I feel the knife slicing through me, blood spurting everywhere.

"You're killin' me! Killin' the baby!" I imagine myself screaming at the doctor, even though I was knocked out when Timothy was born.

In my dreams, I see Timothy drowning in my blood, gasping for air. His pale arms are red, and his fists, when he opens them, are filled with my blood. He tries to cry and gurgles instead, swallowing my beet-red blood, which fed him for nine months. He chokes and coughs, sputters on my blood.

"You're killing the baby. Do something!" I scream at the doctor again, a doctor with no face, only a white coat with a name tag that I can't read from my position lying on my back.

The nurse pulls the baby out, cuts the cord, and suddenly it is I who can't breathe. I am gasping for air like someone with asthma, reaching out to the doctor, grabbing his coat and coming up with thin air. My hand moves through his clothes, and as I scream, I can feel my life draining out of me. I use up my last breath screaming, screaming, and watching the nurses and the doctor watching me die.

I dream that dream the first night my mother comes, after I hear Miss Maisey telling her what I have done. I jump out of bed, suddenly cold. I hear Grams's feet shuffling across the wooden floor long before she reaches my room. She knows without my saying that it is a dream about Timothy. We don't have to talk. She knows I never forget.

I listen to Grams's feet again shuffling away from me. Before Grams is back in bed, I hear the unmistakable creak of the bed as my mother puts her full weight back on the sagging mattress.

# Standfast's Son

⁓

*T*he women's stories, the remains of the bridge, Sonya's
prepackaged grief and her newly found attachment to
Timothy, whose eyes demanded no answers, spurred Sonya's
actions. Without her mother's permission and without asking
about her daughter's plans, Sonya ordered a grave dug next to
her father's, a headstone to be erected the day of the burial and
not months later, as had been done when her father died. She
chose the gray stone herself.

"Standfast's Son" was etched into the top of the stone, "A
brave one who died before he could begin to fight," followed at
the bottom in smaller letters: "Timothy Williams. June
1990–November 1993."

All Friday morning, Sonya watched the men who came to
dig the grave. She dragged a chair from the house and sat

under a mango tree in the yard, fanning flies and mosquitoes away with one hand and holding the other over her brow to hide her tears. She didn't seem to feel the sun, nor see the sweat dripping off the men's sun-darkened bodies. Hourly she raised her body and looked to see how deep and how wide the men had dug the grave. She gave no instructions.

At eleven, Sonya left her post and started a fire to prepare the men's lunch: boiled bananas, yam, and callaloo. She didn't ask her mother for help. She ignored her mother when her mother came to ask why Sonya thought she could do everything her own way.

When the men ate, Sonya didn't eat, nor did she leave her place by the tree. She watched the hole until the men returned to work. She watched the depth of the hole grow to twelve feet and the width to five feet. She thought of her children at three years old, measured their size against the height of her employers' two children, and pictured Timothy's casket being lowered into the hole.

"Too small, too young," she thought.

What she was doing was right, she knew. She thought again of the lives of her two children that she could have ended, but didn't. That was the simple difference between her and her daughter. She found a way, left the child for someone else to raise because she knew she couldn't. If only Kelithe had done the same, the tragedy could have been averted.

Minutes before the men were finished, Teacher Williams's son came by. He avoided the house, seemed to know instinctively that Sonya would be at the back of the house, standing watch as the grave was being dug.

"Miss Maisey sen' me over," he said, fingering his hat in his hand. He smelled of varnish and paint.

"Yes."

"Well, I want to make the casket for the bwoy, if it's alright with you."

"Thanks." Sonya reached into her pocket and pulled out some bills. "Paint it white."

"No, ma'am. I don't need the money, ma'am. I 'ave the paint already."

"Is jus' a little something," Sonya said. She pressed the money into his hand and closed his palm over it.

"Thanks, ma'am. What kin' of material you want inside?"

"What you have?"

"Just a little bit o' red satin. If that alright."

"Yes, red. Red and white."

For the first time in days, Sonya smiled. She smiled, not at Teacher Williams's son but at the fact that her plans for her grandson were coming together. Maisey had talked with the men at the funeral parlor, and they had agreed to prepare the body without charge. Maisey said she would let out the too-small burial suit. Other women had offered to cook whatever they had or help her prepare what she had to make sure the boy went off to his maker without needing to look back and question life.

Teacher Williams's son left the way he had come. Nervous, he glanced at the house and stepped faster as if there was something he had to fear.

Sonya avoided the house, her mother, her daughter. At midafternoon, when the men were done, she remained at her post, watching as if she expected something to happen to the newly dug grave. She was roused only by the sound of a song, the taunt of children:

*Kill you' baby,*
*Watch him drown*
*So you can go a Kingston town.*
*Wouldn't want you for a ma,*
*Wouldn't want you for a pa,*
*You woulda kill me too, like you kill me little bredda.*
*Kill you' baby,*
*Watch him drown,*
*So you can go a Kingston town.*
*Muuurderer, muuurderer!*

The words were sharp, sharper still because they came from the mouths of children. Sonya ran to the front of the yard when she heard her mother shout, "Unno move and go a unno ya'd."

The children ran, their little feet kicking up dust, the girls' blue tunics and white shirts whizzing by, the boys' khaki uniforms blending with the light brown of the dirt road.

"Muurderer, muurderer!" the children started shouting again when they thought they were at a safe distance.

Grams bent to pick up a stone.

"What you doing? A little pickney dem, you know," Sonya shouted and grabbed her mother's hand.

"They don' have no right."

"Children. Is only children. What harm they can do?"

Grams pulled her hand from her daughter's grasp and turned away.

195

Kelithe stepped out into the yard and bent to pick up a stone. She held out her palm to her mother, the stone filling her open palm.

"If you think I guilty, then do what they never do."

Sonya didn't expect such forwardness, didn't even know whether her daughter's act was outside her normal behavior or not. She struggled for words, and when she didn't find any that could counter such a bold and desperate move, she reached instead to knock the stone from her daughter's hand.

"No." Kelithe closed her hands over the stone. "Stone me. Throw it if you think I could do what they say I do." She reopened her hands and bared the stone.

"Kelithe," Grams called. "Kelithe? Leave her."

Kelithe didn't move but waited for her mother's words or action. Sonya didn't look at her daughter's eyes but shifted her gaze instead to the road where the children had run. She thought of the women's pain, the naked shell of the burned-out bridge, the death that made a sleeping town wake up, and knew she had to take the spirit of Standfast in place of her daughter's word.

When Grams reached her granddaughter, Kelithe dropped the stone and turned away from her mother. The stone fell to the soft earth, soundless.

She doesn't love me. She would probably do it. Throw that stone.

My mother. Mom. Mummy.

Of course, what harm can they do? Sticks and stones . . . My mother taught me that long ago. I was four, running home crying because the children I walked home with had teased me about something.

"They're only words," she said.

Standfast's anger is boiling over, erupting like a volcano,

the lava flowing from the town, running toward our house. First the women. The men. Now the children. My mother.

"Father Rapes Daughter." "Father Jailed after 5-Year Incestuous Relationship Revealed." "Grandmother Kills Child in Exorcism Ritual." Headlines like those, and the country does nothing. No town meetings, no demonstrations or rallies. No roadblocks. No uprising. Sometimes calls to the radio station from people asking what the world is coming to. But no anger boiling over and erupting like this. No children singing songs, taunting and teasing, standing firm in the face of rock stones that have no eyes.

My mother doesn't say anything at all.

But I know she would probably stone me. All the trouble I caused her. Her broken windshield. Her pride.

She does not love me.

I wanted her to come. She has come. I wanted her to be my mother, to remember to kiss me good-bye.

She has come but not for me, not to me. She has come, but she does not love me.

How do you stop a heart?

Take your love away. That is the way to slow the beating. Like the way Timothy stopped singing when I left him for a little while. When my mother left, she didn't stop my heart. She left me with a promise that kept me for fifteen years. Timothy stopped singing because he didn't have a promise, didn't have a reason to hope.

Whatever love had been there between my mother and me, my mother has taken away. Or maybe there was never anything there. I was never wanted. Kris is wanted and loved. My sister. The daughter who isn't a burden.

197

My mother has found her reason not to love. She is cold, not at all what I imagined a mother to be. She seems to be calculating, taking it all in, and I wonder when she too will erupt like Standfast has, openly accuse me of killing the grandson she didn't want in the first place.

How do you stop a heart?

Bury a fifteen-year promise. When I was at school, I dreamed of a mother who stayed. A mother involved in my life. A mother who helped me cut out, sew, embroider the aprons, dish towels, skirts we made for sewing class. Who helped me get A's.

I dreamed of touches that signaled love. Words that fell like rain from the top of my head, falling around me like balloons, or bubbles. I imagined those bubble-words when Timothy and I sang at night, how my words, my songs, made him feel loved. I never asked if he dreamed those words at night. But when he slept next to me, he sometimes laughed in his sleep and woke with a smile on his face.

Was I ever in my mother's dreams?

How do you start a heart?

Renew a fifteen-year-old dream. In Standfast you need dreams.

Dream. For you, Timothy, I dream. Lawyer, doctor, Indian chief . . .

Afternoon and evening blended. The clouds didn't lift but hung like a low, oppressive tent. No one in Standfast cared whether it rained or not. The river was full. Green leaves spilled from branches to brush the earth. Goats let loose in the morning to roam returned in the evening with taut, full stomachs.

The cows and pigs were left to fatten, spared a few weeks to ensure richer profits at Christmas.

The health of the land, especially since the Christmas holidays were only four weeks away, should have led to widespread bliss, or at least a softening of hearts. But the sunless afternoon, the quick nightfall, suited Standfast's darkening mood.

Once again Standfast's women walked at night with flickering kerosene lamps. Only this time Sonya was with them. Maisey led the way. The women branched out around Sonya as if she needed protection. The solemn, silent procession made its way to the revival that Maisey had mentioned Thursday night.

They were all dressed in black, some with veils on their heads, others with hats. About fifty women in all, some who were there at the setup the night before, others who had joined along the way to Grams's house. All with one belief: it was time for Standfast to take a stand against something, not sit back anymore and take whatever came.

Sonya felt that she belonged, that she was a part of something. For the first time in her life, she belonged, not to someone but to a place. She didn't belong to New York, nor did she feel completely at home in America. She wore her sadness like a tattoo branded to her face. Her eyes were not sad, nor were they happy.

She didn't think of Kelithe as her daughter, but kept the word "justice" in her mind. She thought, too, of the promises the forefathers had made to fight for justice, whatever the cost. Now, the death of Timothy demanded justice, whatever the cost to Kelithe.

All her youth, Sonya wanted to escape, dreamed of the day

199

she would look back one last time on the town and say good-bye. And when her opportunity had come, she had forgotten numerous things. It was as if she had opened up her suitcase when she arrived in New York and folded in her memories of the Rio Minho; the mud she walked through when the river overflowed its banks and made its power known; the clinging red dirt that stained bare feet. All Standfast viewed her as a foreigner, as one who would look at the river and the green plants growing in abundance next to it and think lush. Sonya was only an ally for the time being, because the town remembered her fifteen-year absence and knew she would be leaving again soon.

Even so, Sonya felt as if she belonged, was for once at one with the town.

# Timothy's Funeral

He's at peace. His body is stiff. There's a slight smile on his face, as if the men who prepared his body were trying to make him laugh, trying to make him look like a child happy to go home to his maker. His arms are folded across his chest, and a small, green New Testament Bible rests in his hands. He looks as if he's about to burst into his bubbly laughter, the sounds breaking into hiccups, the way they usually did whenever he laughed long and hard.

I can think only of the last time I held him, his body limp in my arms, his arms lifeless and hanging by the side of his body. My eyes had filled with tears, and the hot drops had fallen onto his wet shirt. I remember the feel of his limp body, totally dependent on me, like the day he was born. Water was falling from his nose, his mouth, dripping from his wet clothes.

Small pebbles had dropped from his body and from his clothes where they had stuck when the river women had placed his body on the gravel. It was minutes after they had lifted his body from the river.

Now I lift his head first, one palm cradling his head and his neck, my other arm supporting his back, the way I did when he was just days old. Through the cloth, his body is cold, and I remember that his body has been on ice. When I lift him, he's heavy, much heavier than I remember him being, and I fall to the floor holding his weight. Through my dress and thin stockings, the floor, too, is cold, and I shiver from the touch of my baby and the cold floor. Both are sending chills through my body.

His head rests against my breast, right where it should be, and his mouth is soft against my nipple, above my beating heart. But his lips are hard, dry against the softness of my own, and his cheeks are rubbery. His legs don't fall, don't bend at the knees the way they should, and I try bending them, try pushing them to a more natural position. He feels like a doll, too hard to rest comfortably against my body, arms too stiff to curve around my back, neck too rigid to force his head back so his eyes can look on my face.

I think of the day I brought him home, his body tiny and almost helpless, his cry starting small and ending in a wail. His head was covered in a small knitted cap, the first of many things my mother sent for him, with matching socks on his small feet. I remember mostly his tiny fingers grasping my hand, seeking comfort and security, his legs kicking aimlessly with little power. I was amazed then at how much he drank, the power of his lips sucking the milk from my breasts. His body was powerful—his legs, his arms, his lips, his cry. At nights I used to let him sleep in my bed, and I worried that my large body would roll on top of his small one and smother him in the night. I would listen to him breathe, put my hands above his mouth to feel the warm air, and wake before he did to pull the thin sheets back over his body. When he was about five months old, he found my breasts himself. He pushed my nightie aside and sucked until he was full, drifting off to sleep with his head resting against my breast, his tiny hands lying on my chest.

Sometimes I was afraid to touch him, afraid that his body, covered with soap, would slip from my grasp under the soapy water in the basin. I was afraid, too, that my milk would poison him, that the food I ate wouldn't agree with him, that he would throw up or have stomachaches because of my milk. I worried I was too young, not ready to be a mother to my son, Timothy. My baby, Timothy.

I remember the first time he learnt to hug, the first time he placed his arms around my neck and clung to me, not because he thought he was going to fall but because he was mimicking my hugs, showing me he loved me. He had covered my face with kisses, his spit dribbling on my face, and sounds that seemed like words falling from his lips. He would laugh, too, at everything I said, and smile each time I opened my mouth or came into his sight. He would laugh when I told him not to do something, doing it over and over again, to hear my voice, and laughing each time my voice got louder and louder. He didn't     203
laugh with Grams that way. He smiled often but listened when she said no, when she told him to stop doing something that was wrong. He knew I was his mother, the one who brought

him into this world. When he first learned to walk, he used to follow me from room to room, finding a way to drag his body down the steps to the front of the house so he wouldn't lose me when I walked outside. He would stand outside the bathroom door, waiting till I was done, waiting to see my face again. Grams told me, too, that whenever I went away he would sit outside on the steps waiting till I came back. And when I did return, he was always there, arms outstretched, smile wide on his face. I loved that feeling of always turning around and knowing that he was there, not running away from me but running toward me, ready to hold my legs for comfort.

My warm tears now fall on his cold body, on the suit I pressed stiff with starch. The funeral parlor director did as I told him and folded his hands in front. But I forgot that bent elbows swallow some of the material. Anyone looking on closely will notice the suit's sleeves are a little short. His shoes, the black penny loafers I had bought for him to wear to school, fit just fine. They covered his face with brown powder, some of which is rubbing off on my dress, standing out against the black material.

The mended suit fits him fine. And he's a sweet baby, handsome and at peace. I sing a song for him, one that I don't know if my mother ever sang for me: "Rock a bye, baby, on the tree top / When the wind blows the cradle will rock / When the bough breaks the cradle will fall / And down will come baby, cradle and all."

I sing softly for his ears only, for my only baby. I sing him the Twenty-third Psalm. He likes that one.

The hands on my shoulders aren't soft. Warm, but not soft. There are other warm hands touching my wrists, pulling my hands away from my baby. They're taking my son away from me again, these river women. They're prying my arms from around his body, pulling me from the front of the church. It's like that first day, the day my son died when none of the women wanted to let me get near my son's body. I should have gone someplace else, somewhere quiet to spend these last few minutes alone with my son.

I feel liquid when I clamp down on an arm, and when I look up it's my mother's face that is twisted in pain, her lips that are stretched wide, her teeth that are stark white against bright red lipstick. Her eyes are closed tightly, and when she reopens them she looks first at me and pulls my son's body from my arms. With one movement his heavy body is back in the casket, his head raised on the pillow, and his body lying against the satin covering the insides of the casket.

"Get up, girl," she says through clenched teeth. "The funeral 'bout to start, and you not embarrassing me no more. You better stop this foolishness. You hear me? Stop it."

She looks as if she's about to slap me. Her right arm is raised, her palm open, her fingers standing straight, curving slightly backward, as if they've been banded together. Her face is close to mine. I can feel her breath against my lips, and then briefly against my cheeks, as she bends a little to look quickly down at the drops of blood spurting up from the place where my nails have dug into her arm. Her eyes are narrow when she looks up at me again. She looks as if she's ready to fight. And I think that I want to fight back too.

But I feel like I've been running for a long time. My body is tired, drained, and I'm breathing as if I have been running and am out of breath. My legs hurt, either from the pressure of

205

Timothy's heavy body pressing my legs onto the cold floor, or because I had kept them bent for so long. And because I'm weak, tired, I don't fight back. I get up, feeling again how cold the floor is.

Grams bends in front of me, pulls my arm, and brushes her fingers across my face. It is on her shoulder that I lean as we walk back to the pews.

My mother sits behind me, and Grams and I are directly in front of Timothy's casket, directly under the gaze of the pastor and the choir. The pastor is looking at me. I'm not sure what to think or what he's thinking. It looks like he is smiling at me or about to break into laughter. I imagine all eyes boring into the back of my head, much like the eyes from the choir in front of me, and I rest my head on the back of the bench in front of me and cry silently.

"He looks like such a sweet angel," I hear someone say to my mother. "So sorry, ma'am."

"He's at peace. God rest his soul."

"Such a short life, eh?"

"When God calls, you know, nothing you can do but answer."

"I wish it was better circumstances you come back home under. Nobody like come back home from foreign to bury the dead."

I turn my head to see the wife of the deacon from the Pentecostal church that is across the street from our Baptist church. She looks away from my face back to my mother's wrinkling face, stretching out her hand at the same time to pat my mother on her back. My mother is mourning the grandson she never wanted in the first place, receiving the well wishes I should be receiving. The women greet Grams, too, whispering words of comfort and patting her on her back. But they ignore me, the invisible, lifeless mother that I am.

It's a packed church for the Saturday-afternoon funeral. Full black church. Death everywhere. Nobody wears purple or even white. It's not a market day. Hasn't been a market day since the day Timothy died, since the day Standfast started protesting. They've taken time off today to mourn my son, but the roadblocks are still standing. Today the fires have stopped burning. They've opened up a place, a narrow path for the hearse, the other cars, and the mourners on foot to pass through. My mother is the chosen one, the honored one, today. Not like when they stoned the car, breaking the glass and nearly hitting my mother in the head.

My mother gives the eulogy. When the minister calls her name, she takes her time walking up the narrow aisle, one hand on the top of the pews as if she can't walk without support.

She knows nothing about Timothy, but she stands in front of the packed church to sing praises about her dead grandson. She measured his growth only by the size of the clothes he wore, how quickly he would grow out of a pair of pants, a soft baby shoe. She didn't see his first steps, feel the sharpness of his first teeth, hear him say "peanup" instead of peanut, see the happiness in his eyes when he got a word right. She didn't see his smile the first time he held a soft baby chick in his hands or the first time he saw a chicken lay an egg and then asked me why he couldn't do the same. No, my mother doesn't know her grandson, so she sings his praises the best way she knows how.

207

She tells the church what they already know and maybe what they don't already know.

She tells the story of Moses, the story of that baby floating gently in a basket made of bush. Reeds, the Bible says. She is the mother of Moses who saved her child from sure death by putting him in a basket under the watchful eye of his sister. My mother describes herself as Moses' mother, the mother who found a good solution, setting her daughter, who she says probably wouldn't have survived very well in an American city, away from her. What's important, she tells the mourners, is that she put me under the watchful eye of her own mother, a place safer than the streets of New York City.

My mother forgets that I was saved from my grandfather's persecution, saved because my grandfather didn't kill the growing baby inside my mother when he found out that his young daughter was pregnant. Grams is the pharoah's daughter, the one who saved me, not once, but twice. She stepped in to raise me when my mother went off without me, saving me from the mother who didn't love me enough to take me with her to that other place.

My mother doesn't mention that she nearly killed me herself, or that Grams was the one who saved me from her attempt at an abortion.

"Timothy could have been that baby Moses, sailing in a basket, under the watchful eyes of somebody who loved him," she says, ending her eulogy.

208　　The preacher shakes her hand, holds her close, and wipes away her tears. Out of the corner of my eye, I see Grams's face, set like a stone, hard. She doesn't seem to blink. She doesn't turn her head when my mother nears our pew. I look my mother in the eye, waiting to see the tears that have collected above her lids flowing down her face. Her vision might be blurred, but she sees the hands stretched out to her, reaches out to touch the ones that are closer to the edge of the benches.

"The little angel in heaven looking down," she says to the church, acknowledging their sympathy. "Yes, that little boy turned angel is looking down."

When my mother settles herself, Grams leaves. Her shoes make no noise, but their eyes follow her. I follow. She walks, but I run. I run because my legs are carrying me, lifting higher and higher even though I want to hold them to the ground, fall on my knees, curl up and cry. Cry for my lost son, lost mother. A mother who has no words for me, but who can take my only son from me and weave his memory as her own, Standfast's own. I don't want them to see me cry, to think they have broken me.

I run because there is nothing for me here, nothing holding me back in this town where a preacher can chase a grieving mother out of a church, where a mother can hold her daughter up like she would hold up a witch waiting to be hung. Nothing for me here where I'll never live a dream, any dream, because my son's face is stamped in the hatred of these people who will never let me live or love again.

# The Burial

⁓

*F*our women carried the white casket. Sonya followed, looking as regal and as matronly as she had looked the night the women poured out their hearts to her at the impromptu wake. Her hair was wrapped in a black scarf flecked with gold. She wore a jacket, a long black skirt, off-black sheer stockings, and high heels. Maisey held Sonya's right arm. David Daniels, member of Parliament representing the district, held Sonya's other arm. Sonya's white handkerchief fluttered like a white flag, like a sign of peace. Sometimes she bent her head and dabbed her eyes, but mostly she kept her head high as if she had to keep watch, keep out those who didn't belong with the funeral procession.

All Standfast turned out—the river women; the children who had stoned Sonya's car, unapologetic but present for her and Timothy's benefit; Teacher Williams and the men who had come with him to the wake; Hush Puppies. There were faces Sonya had long scratched out from her memory, men who reminded her of her father and grandfather, wistful faces that reminded her of her own desperate childhood dreams about escape; children who looked at her longingly, as if by staring hard they could take from her some of what they wished for themselves. Those children she wanted to pull close and whisper to them her secret.

"Dream," she would tell them. "Dream big."

She was perhaps their age—seven or eight years old—when she started dreaming of her fairy-tale endings. It began in the summer, the hot days when young, idle hands were taken to help her father with farming. She walked behind her father, stepping where he stepped, and dropped pea grains into the holes he had dug. There was always another child behind her—the son or daughter of the man who had come to help her father plant—who covered the red peas with soil. When the peas were ready, the whole family gathered to stomp open the dried pods, to separate the good peas from those eaten by worms or weevils. Those weren't memories she would forget.

"Think of the ending," she would say. "Johnny got the gold from the River Mumma because he kept on thinking of the end, the good part of the story. Your mothers and fathers still here 'cause they can't forget Standfast's one failure long enough to think about the happy ending."

There, too, lay her primary criticism of Kelithe. She didn't think her daughter was farsighted enough to look beyond the past, the immediate years without Timothy, and concentrate on the happy ending to come. For Sonya, it had been easy; as long as she could remember, that was the way she had approached things. She wanted others to be that way, too, to be independent and strong enough to adopt an approach like hers.

Sonya resented Kelithe, too, and could so readily stand with the other women because she wanted to believe that Kelithe's shortsightedness had led to the death of her grandson. Because of his mother's shortsightedness, the boy was cheated of his opportunity to dream of the happy endings to come.

Sonya looked for Kelithe and Grams and was secretly happy she didn't see either of the two. Although she had stood up before the church and blamed her daughter for Timothy's death, she wasn't sure what she would have said, how she would have acted, in the presence of her daughter and her own mother. Sonya knew Grams would have ignored her. Or cut her eyes. Perhaps she would have created an accident and bounced her body or stepped on her toe, deliberately forgetting to apologize. Whatever the action, Grams's response would have been definite.

She couldn't say the same for Kelithe. The sharp press of Kelithe's fingers into her arm was like a vine growing in her mind. Her arm still tingled. But the image in her mind was the openness of Kelithe's eyes, the almost childlike innocence reflected there when Kelithe lifted her eyes from Timothy's stiff body to hers so high above the ground. Kelithe's questioning eyes remained. Vivid. Haunting. Discomfiting.

She was thankful for the MP's presence. She thought his attendance justified her actions, the town's reaction. She was even more grateful for his steadying grasp because without his holding her arm, she would certainly have fallen at least one of the numerous times her feet wobbled on the uneven road.

The MP made no public promises. He presented himself at Timothy's funeral, on Standfast's side, because his absence would have been more noticeable than his presence. He came because those who relied on the main road that Standfast had blocked expected their MP to restore the order that Standfast had disrupted. The river women read his presence as a promise of justice to come and raised their voices higher. The women treated him like a lost son finally come home, like one who had brought a bag of gold to be evenly distributed to those who still believed.

But the MP knew his role. He played it well.

He asked Sonya's permission to set up a fund in Timothy's name that would go toward educating young parents. He wanted to tell young mothers of common things that are dangerous to children—buckets of water; easily accessible bottles of kerosene or bleach; plastic shopping bags that can cling to a child's face and prevent air from reaching the nose; matches; improperly balanced dressers that can tip over; self-locking doors. He repeated "buckets of water" when he could think of no tactful way to say "river." The MP whispered so only Sonya heard his words.

Next, the MP told her he would talk to the police in charge of the local station, see why nothing had been done and what could now be done. "Maybe nothing. But if something like this or any other crime occurs, the police must respond. The people must know that the police will respond."

213

Sonya nodded, patted the MP's hand as if the words were not meant to comfort her. When the MP ran short of promises for Sonya, the three—Sonya, Maisey, the MP—walked in silence. After a time the MP gently lowered Sonya's arm and dropped back to someone else.

To Teacher Williams, the MP promised to request a new school, new textbooks, a school lunch program. The MP said he wanted to provide an incentive to the young children, reasons for them to learn not just about the Arawaks who gave the country its poetic name, the Spaniards who renamed the places the Arawaks had settled, and the British who came to claim what the Spanish had previously taken from the Arawaks. But he wanted the children to learn to dream, to earn a place among the national heroes. He put Teacher Williams in charge of determining a name for the new school. "Someone the town would want to honor."

Whether Teacher Williams believed the MP or not, he patted the MP's hand and mouthed his thanks.

"Another time I'll think 'bout that," Teacher Williams said. "But Standfast thank you anyway."

The two men walked side by side, both sharply observant.

The MP saw the burned remains of the bridge.

Teacher Williams observed the charred remains of the bridge as a symbol of a promise now buried.

The MP noticed that the road had never been paved.

Teacher Williams noticed potholes that were long overdue for a refilling and told himself to remember to gather the men for the job.

The MP thought he now understood the way poverty eroded pride.

Teacher Williams marveled at how his people remained mindful of all the neighbors.

The MP wondered how long it would take for the young people to leave, seek a life elsewhere.

Teacher Williams saw a new beginning for Standfast.

Of Miss Maisey, MP Daniels asked what she thought Standfast most needed.

Miss Maisey looked him over. First she trained her eyes on his polished black shoes, his pants of perfect length, his jacket flapping open against a rounded stomach.

"Wha' we need, we have." Miss Maisey spoke grudgingly, as if her words were reserved for someone else. "See all de people here. Da's wha' we need. People who believe in themself. And don' trus' nobody to do t'ings for dem."

Miss Maisey looked over the rest of the MP, from his head to his neck.

"You a politician, a sweet talker. Dat we don' need."

Although the bridge, the last physical reminder of the long-lost promise, was gone, Miss Maisey didn't want to forget that Standfast had banked its future on a rescinded government promise and lost. She didn't trust outsiders, grudgingly trusted Sonya, whom she now thought of as an outsider. But she had to trust Sonya because she was the only person who could prevent Kelithe, whom Miss Maisey thought of as a merciless killer, from escaping her punishment.

The younger women, for whom the story of the bridge had become a folktale, welcomed the MP and viewed his presence as a sign of change. The town had unwittingly burned the bridge that not only served a pedestrian purpose but also marked the town's rootedness in the past. What the younger women wanted to take from the past was the readiness of their ancestors to fight for their land. It was those ready, willing traits that fueled the response to Timothy's death, the roadblocks, Pam's trek to the police station, the ultimate riot that led to the burning of the bridge.

The willing spirits prevailed. Pam presented the MP with a list of the women's demands. Running water. Electricity. Asphalted roads. Two bus stops on the main road. A health clinic. More frequent visits from a public health nurse. A police investigation into Timothy's death. Prosecution of Kelithe.

"In honor of Timothy," was written beneath. They couldn't forget Standfast's isolation, the numerous elections that had come and gone without a politician entering the town or dispatching a road work crew to show the town residents their representative had the town in mind. Because of the circumstances of the death, the women wanted to believe that any promise made in Timothy's honor would be kept. They desperately wanted to cling to the idea of something good coming from what they termed the sacrifice of Timothy.

The MP listened. He nodded, said he would see what he could do.

The women nodded, too. Hopeful. Empowered.

Sonya led the silent procession through the gate, into her mother's yard. They walked by the side of the house near the road. Kelithe was sitting in a chair by the open grave, her eyes trained steadily at the dark hole. The sunlight didn't reach far within the hole. She didn't move. Even her eyelids seemed frozen.

Sonya held up her palm, and the crowd stopped as if it had

anticipated something just like this. Sonya knew she couldn't question Kelithe's presence at her own son's burial. The spirit that had overtaken Sonya while she was eulogizing Timothy, that presented itself when she was closely surrounded by the women, that she had borrowed from the women the night they staged the setup, left her. She felt the presence of her body, as if someone had walked up behind her and pushed her into the swirling Rio Minho, against which her entire body had to struggle.

"Kelithe watched him drown and never do anything to help." She rehashed what the women had said and the events that solidified her acceptance of the river women's story.

Behind her the women lowered the casket and waited. A few people moved forward. Miss Maisey stepped away from the crowd and approached Sonya. The MP made a move, but the preacher held him back. Sonya kept her eyes on her daughter's back, without acknowledging Maisey. Sonya stepped away from the light touch on her arm. She didn't look back to see if her friend had retreated. But she heard the low rise of the singing voices from the previously silent group.

Sonya wondered about Grams. But she knew her mother, once she turned away and walked out of the church, wouldn't return. Grams held grudges long, made sure her displeasure showed. Still, Sonya was surprised her mother hadn't come to take Kelithe away.

Could she have been wrong? Could she have misread her daughter, Standfast, so completely? Sonya hesitated, waited for the crowd behind her to support her, press forward, drown out Kelithe's words. "Go with your gut feeling," she remembered Maisey saying.

217

Slowly Kelithe raised her head in the direction of her mother. Her eyes no longer queried. Neither were her eyes the red, swollen eyes of a person who had recently cried. They were steady, like the practiced eyes of a judge bellowing out a punishment.

"Tell me to leave." Kelithe stood, her stare level with her mother's. Her voice was not loud, but rising from so deep within that she almost sounded masculine.

Kelithe waited for a response.

Sonya wanted the crowd behind her to look at the exchange and consider her the stronger of the two, since she refused to be drawn into a quarrel at the open grave site. Inside, answers to the questions she suspected Kelithe would ask churned. She started to answer. But Kelithe shushed her, brought a single finger so close to Sonya's lip that Sonya moved forward instinctively to complete the touch.

"No, don't tell me. I want to know all the answers. From way back then to this." Briefly Kelithe looked behind her at the crowd, and then at the open hole. "But don't tell me.

"Fifteen years." Kelithe spread her fingers as if the words were a weight she wanted to let fall through the open spaces. "Fifteen years. And this is what I get. My mother chasing me from my own son's funeral. Go on then and *tell* me to leave."

Kelithe walked around her mother and to the women standing at the four corners of the white casket. "I want to bury my son."

Kelithe bent forward to take the casket and probably would have dragged it on the ground had not the women bent to pick it up.

"*I* want to bury my son." Kelithe repeated her words, her

voice again so deep it sounded as if she had pushed all the air in her body to the pits of her stomach to force the words out.

The women lowered the casket and stepped back. Kelithe bent forward. She stopped for a moment, straightened her back, and measured the distance to the open hole. She bent again and tested the weight of the casket. She moved quickly. The women stood back and then moved to take their place behind Sonya.

"Let us go on." The minister stepped forward. He bellowed the first words of a prayer.

"You already did your part," Kelithe said. She didn't raise her eyes from the white casket on the ground.

The minister cleared his throat and continued. Sonya stepped closer to Kelithe, strengthened now by the presence of the women near. She held on to Kelithe's arm, her fingers pressing into Kelithe's flesh like a too-small bangle.

"I want to bury my son," Kelithe repeated, as if those were the only words she knew.

The minister stopped again. This time he didn't look at Kelithe but at Sonya, because he wanted her to take back control the way she had in the church. Sonya's fingers pressed deeper into Kelithe's arm.

"For peace sake, girl, stop it." Her voice was low but fierce.

Kelithe turned slowly and gently lifted her mother's fingers. "For peace sake," she said in return. "Let *me* bury my son." She didn't let go of her mother's fingers but pressed hard, squeezing the bones and flesh until Sonya twisted her arm to release herself. Sonya's body twisted, too. But she refused to let out her pain.

The women behind Sonya rustled as if they wanted to say

or do something but didn't have the courage. The MP stepped up and took his place beside Sonya again. He lowered his head to her ear, in the conspiratorial way he had spoken to her previously about setting up the fund in honor of Timothy.

"She the mother, right?" he asked. "She has as much right to be here. For Timothy's sake." He added the last when Sonya shook her head. Those were the key words. Anything, for Timothy's sake.

The MP said the same to the minister.

"But we have to get the body in the grave. Now you want her to do work of God?"

"You're a man of God. Let God and the law take care of the judging. She the mother. Let her mourn."

The MP stood next to Kelithe.

"He liked to sing," Kelithe said. "My son used to like to sing."

To the crowd, he said, "Continue to sing your praises to the Lord. In honor of Timothy."

The MP and Kelithe lowered the casket. Kelithe looked at it for a long time. Sonya didn't watch the lowering of the casket, tried hard to drown out the sounds of stone and dirt falling on the wood. She watched the setting sun, the rustling leaves, the bodies of the women swaying to the beat of their songs. She remembered her father's burial, Grams leaning on her right side for support, a young Kelithe on the left side reaching across to wipe her tears.

220    Kelithe sprinkled a handful of dust, listened to the hollow sound of small stones hitting the wood. "Tell them to leave it open," she said to the MP before she walked away through the crowd and into her grandmother's house.

The minister took back his rightful place. Sonya stood tall again. Standfast proceeded.

While the men mixed the cement for the vault, the MP left Sonya's side. The minute he stepped away, she missed his presence; the warmth from his body reminded her of that long-ago time when her mother and daughter stood on either side of her as her father's casket was lowered. His presence reminded her as well of the women who had rallied to her side and attended to her in a manner she had never before experienced.

The MP moved to the center of the mourners. "This is an end." He glanced at the men, the mound of watery, gray cement. "But it is also a beginning."

*Yeas* rose up from the crowd and floated like birds overhead. Each utterance appeared to linger and disappear only when another sound rose up. The sounds joined back to back like a round being sung. Sonya marveled at the unity, something she had never before witnessed in Standfast, and wished now that she truly belonged to that circle.

"Today, I heard what people here desire most—running water, electricity, roads, a school." When Sonya heard that sentence, she imagined the MP's words traveling directly at her at the speed of the mighty Rio Minho and landing with a thud in the middle of her chest. "It is a beginning because from a death has come so much energy. A new life to Standfast!"

Sonya stumbled over the rocks as if her feet had indeed been slapped by wave after wave of water. The events of the past week played over and over, and she combed each day's actions for clues to the truth she thought was now unraveling, what she now believed: these river women would do anything, much like her, to change the circumstances of their lives. And in that realization lay another. Daughter, like mother, probably would do anything to change the circumstances of her life.

Somewhere in all of this the truth was hidden, its heavy presence settling the way sediment does on the bottom of a river, to be uncovered only if the river goes dry or if a dredge is used to clean the riverbed. She hadn't asked Kelithe what had occurred, and now she couldn't.

Sonya stood alone between the group surrounding the MP and her mother's house. Not welcome by either.

# Sonya's Final Departure

It's like it was the first day she came. Polite quiet from my mother. Not the quiet of waiting. Not the forced silence of boarding-school dining tables or afternoon prep. Not the quiet in the car on the day she took me home from school, concentrating on handling the car's steering wheel. It's the quiet of knowing the answer, the quiet of the principal sitting behind her desk and waiting for me to tell her, "No, I'm not pregnant," even though she's staring at my belly straining against my uniform and already knows that something is not right.

She is packing quickly, ignoring the breadfruits Grams roasted and then scraped to get the burned black skin off. She doesn't touch the half-ripe pears that Grams wrapped in foil, the peeled sugarcane in the plastic bag, the bottle of hot peppers in vinegar, or the bottle of rum. I don't know why Grams bothered with the food. It must be her way of saying her final farewell. Grams doesn't forgive easily. What my mother did is not a thing to be forgiven.

She remembers her clothes, spread out on the piece of zinc to dry, and folds the stiff pieces of cloth one by one.

Her packing is like the first day she left, years and years ago. I remember burying my head in her skirt, wanting to fold myself in her half-empty suitcase. She didn't carry many clothes, and the clothes she left, Grams tore up and used to wipe up around the house and rub the wood floors. One day she was here and then she was gone, her suitcase full, my heart full of excitement at the going away but not knowing how to measure soon, soon I'll send for you. The soon-soon that has no bottom.

Packing doesn't take long this time. There's no hurry, no rush to buy the hair oil that Grams says she'll never find over foreign. No rush to find the fish that won't break when it's fried. No hurry for dried pimento and thyme that Aunt Berry asked for in her letter. No hurry to find bammy or fresh hard-dough bread, still warm from the oven, to eat with the fish. No rush to take the coconut off the stove before the sugar dries out and the coconut drops dry out and don't stick. No rushing to Maisey for the dress that still had pins in it the night before. No rush to straighten out her hair or set the plastic rollers just right. No rush for the tiny straw basket that Grams says she must keep on her dresser to remind her of home. No hurry to have everything ready before the taxi driver comes by. No rush, no rush.

But not slow.

She ignores Grams and me, and Grams ignores her, too. I want her to say what she hasn't said since she came, to ask the Why? or the Did you? I want her to give me the answers I told her to hold on to. But she keeps her eyes away from the door of the room, and I stand waiting, waiting like the years I waited for soon to turn to now, the kind of waiting I didn't want Timothy to ever know.

The locks of her suitcase snap into place, loud clicks in the quiet house.

Click, click, I think Timothy would say. Or maybe he would reach for the locks to click them into place himself, over and over until the lock broke or he tired of the clicking sounds and moved on to something else. That was what he would have done at two, at three. What would he have done at four and five? Is that what he would have done if I were packing to leave him? Would he have played with the clicking thing and remembered me by the clicking sounds my suitcase made?

The last clicks are her shoes against the floor. Click, then clack. Mostly clack.

She doesn't look around the room for anything left behind. Not the way I looked back when she came to take me away from school. But I looked back because I really wanted to stay, wanted to be anywhere but Standfast.

Clack, clack.

"Bye, Mama. I'll call the post office and sen' a message when I reach."

She bends to kiss Grams's cheek, but Grams only turns her head slightly so her mouth doesn't touch my mother's cheek. I don't know what my mother expected. Grams hasn't spoken to her since Timothy's burial.

225

"Good-bye, Kelithe," I want her to say. "Good-bye." I want the finality of the word. There's no promise in it.

She doesn't kiss me good-bye. But this time it's not because she forgot.

Her leaving is like it was the first time she left, only this time I'm not looking through a glass painted blue trying to see her back. I can see her face clearly through the car's clean glass windows. Her face is a little out of shape because of the crack in the front windshield spiraling out like a cobweb. She doesn't smile as she waves her final good-bye.

It might not even be a wave. It's too quick to be a wave. A flash of her fingers. Her face is set hard, set even more firmly by the deep-brown powder she brushed onto her face. Grams doesn't bother to move from her seat on the verandah. My fingers wave, not because I'm happy or sad to see her go. Her head is turned slightly as she moves the car backward out of the yard. She touches the horn gently, and the slight beep is what I hear, what I'll remember forever of my mother's final departure.

# Dead Sea

⌒

I come to the place of forgetting. No. The place of remembering. Empty of laughter, chatter, the unique sound of cloth and soap and water together, work songs, love songs from the radio, riddles, jokes. No screams from children splashing around in the water. Peace. A peace as quiet as death. Only Rio Minho exists. Dancing like a snake, livelier than a mongoose surrounded by chickens. Pulling in everything and giving off only a chorus that sounds like a thousand nos. No.

He was here, under this tree, stretched out in a peaceful sleep, his head on a brown root that jutted out like a natural pillow. There were no children for him to play with, and he went to sleep instead. There were no ants, neither big nor small. None of the tiny red ants with bites like fire. I checked. And I checked again. No land crabs. No near-dead branches about to fall. I threw a thin shirt over his legs and another over his arms to protect him from mosquitoes and flies. He was fine, as peaceful as if he were in his own bed at home.

Every now and then I looked up. He hadn't shifted at all. He was still curled, his legs up to his chest, one hand stretched out, the other probably under his head. He seemed so much at peace. And I thought again how hard it would be to leave him even for a few months. I was still angry at Miss Maisey for her thoughtless words. Heartless woman, Grams would have said if it had been somebody else. I was sad. But still I was happy because the future held promise. My third escape from Standfast. Third and final. Permanent. An opportunity to start afresh without a history. To not always be known as the worthless girl who went off to school and came back pregnant. To never again be known as that girl. To have a new opportunity similar to the Ministry of Education's push to resettle teen mothers in schools a great distance away from the one they attended when they got into trouble.

Timothy was there. Near that cacoon vine. Before he lay down, he picked up one of the large pods that had fallen from the tree and shook it to hear the rattling of the beans inside. He picked up two of the beans that had fallen from another pod. He held up the beans away from the shade of the vine and rubbed them together. That's what he did when he held any kind of dry bean, whether red peas or gungo. Once I made him a bracelet with the dried beans from the cacoon pod. He only wore it for the sound and moved his hand up and down and left and right to hear the music of the beans rubbing against each other. I promised to make him a shaker, like the ones they use in churches, filled with those beans.

I do what he did that day and rattle a dry pod in one hand and loose beans in the other. The rattle of the beans in the pod mingles with the roars and splashes of the Rio Minho. Meaningless sounds. He was here in this spot, curled like this with the bean pod in one hand and the seeds in the other. Sleeping. At peace.

And then he was here. Not moving. Water running from his eyes, ears, mouth, nose, dripping from his shirt. No. It wasn't there. It was here. Closer to the edge of the river where they laid him down. No. It can't be. I was here spreading a sheet on this stone, away from the sand. Pam was there. Lisette was over there by that big rock. She had sheets spread on the rock and her son's clothes in a basin at her feet. Nobody was in the water. So he must have been here in this spot. I remember running, the clap of my feet on the sand. He couldn't have been too close to me. My heart was racing, and I was breathing heavy when I got to him.

I need to mark the spot. The place where my son's spirit left his body. I make a circle of stones. I don't know what my circle means. Circle: unity, one, togetherness. At school, we sometimes prayed in circles. The guidance counselor always made us form circles for her sessions. And the Girl Guides sat in circles. A full life is a circle. Not Timothy's life. His was too short.

The sand is warm against my back. That's the way he should feel. Warm. Soft. This is where my son last lay. With the sun directly on his face. The *shush-shush* of the river near his ear. Only it couldn't have been *shush-shush* to him. What did he hear before he gave his last breath?

I don't remember his last words to me. I remember him

singing when we crossed the bridge, his questions about America. He was sleepy when we got here, and he lay down and closed his eyes. Maybe he said something then before I turned away from him and the cacoon vine. There couldn't have been any birds around. I don't remember him imitating their song. To not remember his last words. To live forever not knowing his last words, last thoughts, what made him go into water he didn't like, whether he was trying to sneak up and surprise me.

To live with knowing my mother's heartless ways, the ways of the people of Standfast. To live remembering my mother always, always going away from me.

No matter what they say, I know my son is in the Dead Sea, that lifeless body of water is where all the dead go. Why else would they call it that? The cities of Sodom and Gomorrah are buried under there, where dead people have a purpose—holding the live bodies on the water, letting them float. Never sinking. Never drowning. At nights the dead collect the salt, piling it into mounds for the daytime workers who come to mine the salt. They have a purpose there, and when I die I'll join my son in the Dead Sea. Not in heaven or hell. Not in the fire of hell that preachers can describe so eloquently. Or enjoying the angelic peace of nature. No. Swimming always in the Dead Sea and collecting salt at night. Collecting salt and holding up the bodies of children. Preventing another child from being pulled under water and dying the way Timothy died.

The Dead Sea. That's where my son is, and where I want to be when I die.

If not the Dead Sea, then I want to go to some other place where my life is worth more than it is worth here, where what I do is worth something to somebody, where nobody will leave me behind because I'm too much load to carry.

Water is his. Rio Minho is his. His life began here, for it was here, along the bank of the river, that he was conceived. Not far from the spot where he died. When I was pregnant, I used to come here. At first because I couldn't forget his father and wanted to sit in the place we had been so I could remember him. Later, I came because I liked the sound of the water, the spray that kissed my face when I sat on the bank and let my feet hang over the edge. If I hadn't been too scared of the dark and hadn't been concerned about how Grams would worry, I would have slept here in the nights with the sound of the water at my ears. Sometimes I think she followed me and watched to see what I did. But she never said a word.

I love this river's odor, that combined smell of fish and wet things rotting. It is not pleasant to some, and I like it because of that. Not many would sit here like me, in the shadows of trees and on moist ground that will never be truly dry.

I want to swim Rio Minho's width. That's not a thing I've done since that one time with Timothy's father. Without him there to watch and guide me, I lost my nerve and worried that I would get halfway across and not be able to complete the distance. I wanted to teach Timothy to swim. To give him a way to connect with his father, who said he wanted to swim professionally. But Timothy didn't like water.

I crave the cool water tumbling over my body, a complete immersion. A baptismal soaking. I need to be cleaned, made whole.

And this is what I will do. I will stand here where Timothy must have stood. And feel the way the water wrapped around his legs, waist, and covered his head. I will move my arms the way he must have moved his, find how he must have clawed at the water. He must have opened his mouth to call my name, Mommy, Mommy. I want to understand.

I will do this because water is his. Now mine. Always. *Shush-shush.* Always in my ears. Now and forevermore. Shush.

# River Woman

## Donna Hemans

### A Readers Club Guide

# About This Guide

The suggested questions are intended to help your reading group find new and interesting angles and topics for discussion for Donna Hemans's *RIVER WOMAN*. We hope that these ideas will enrich your conversation and increase your enjoyment of the book.

Many fine books from Washington Square Press feature Readers Club Guides. For a complete list, or to read the Guides online, visit http://www.BookClubReader.com.

# Reading Group Questions and Topics for Discussion

1. The lines between mother and child are often blurred in this story, as many of those who give birth are mere children themselves. Look at the ways that the women of Standfast mother each other, the town, and their loved ones. In what ways does this communal sense of mothering shape, alter, and create the town? Are there negative aspects to this type of child rearing?

2. Discuss setting in this novel. How does the hot, dry, stagnant environment work with the plot? The author peppers her prose with adjectives, many of which are so visceral that they border on disturbing. In what ways does this exacerbate the high level of emotional intensity of this novel?

3. Men have a somewhat elusive role in this novel. They are often presented as peripheral to central scenes and, as characters, react more than act, aid more than lead, and watch more than participate. Why does this seem to be the case? Is it simply because the story is told through the point of view of a family of women that men are relegated to the sidelines? Do you see male roles shifting as the novel progresses?

4. On page 176, during the bridge-burning scene, the narrator states, "The young women shattered the symbol that had kept the elder folks mired in the past and waiting for their government to hand out a future. The young women took charge." Why does the author call attention to the fact that it is

the women who finally act out? Is this somehow representative of the ways that women, in the face of absent males, seem to dominate the world of this novel? How do you account for the fact that women, who usually maintain roles as creators, are responsible for so much destruction in this story?

5.   There is the sense that it takes time, patience, and caring to be a good mother, a luxury that neither Sonya nor Kelithe had—seeing as how neither of them were old enough to grow into that. As such, do you think there are mitigating circumstances that may help explain the way that they neglected or abandoned their children? To what extent do you judge the women for their actions?

6.   In the world of Standfast the past never really goes away. Memories of wrongs, both on a personal level and a public level, affect the people of the town deeply, making it impossible for them to ever move on or to ever break free from the bitterness that holds them. And it is only in the ultimate action of destruction and rebellion that the people seem somehow freed from their past. Are there parallels between the destruction of the bridge and the way that Kelithe allegedly lets her son die? How might these parallels demonstrate the disappointment over lost potential and resentment that plague the people of Standfast? If the burning of the bridge was a symbolic break from the past for the townsfolk, how should we view Timothy's death?

7.   The women of Standfast are outraged that Kelithe, at least in their eyes, let her son die—so much so that his death becomes an obsession for the townsfolk, and takes on a life of its own. Why is it that they see the boy's death as a personal affront, even though they are not family? How might the fol-

lowing quote from page 151 shed light on this question? "It was as if each woman brought her painful past, as if by telling her story she was being healed." In what way do the women of Standfast need to be healed?

8. It seems that Kelithe affirms for the women of Standfast their visions of themselves as good mothers. No matter how poorly they may have treated their children, they never let them die. Even Sonya, Kelithe's own mother, often compares her sins with her daughter's, reassuring herself that, although she tried to abort Kelithe, she did not succeed, and therefore should not be subject to the same judgment. In what ways do you see the women of this novel trying to overcome, forget, or overshadow their own infanticidal desires with their harsh criticism of Kelithe?

9. On page 163, Kelithe decides that she could never tell Timothy that something would happen "soon" because "soon" spelled backwards is "noos(e)." Discuss the ways that endless waiting and anticipation squelches the dreams of the characters in this story. To what extent are their actions simply a result of the frustrations that they feel?

10. There is the sense that Sonya's ultimate abandonment of Kelithe comes when she joins the collective grief of Standfast in mourning the death of her grandson—and also when she fails to believe that her daughter is innocent of the crime of which she is accused. How and why does Sonya instinctively join them, rather than her daughter, in her grief? Why does she feel that the town somehow needs her to side with them in their judgment of Kelithe and why does she ultimately decide to betray her own flesh and blood?

11. The author does an interesting thing when she

switches points of view at different times in the novel. How does hearing this story told by different characters, who have different agendas, different opinions, and different ways of seeing the world, affect your ability to ever truly understand what really happened that day by the river? Do you think that the idea of subjectivity is a concept with which the author plays? How would this story have been different had it been told by one character, or if it were told in third-person omniscient?

12. Did you come away from this story with a firm sense of whether or not Kelithe let Timothy die? What do you think her mother or her grandmother thinks? To have an understanding of this novel, is it necessary to know? How about the last chapter? Did it clear anything up for you, or create more questions?

13. The imagery of the final scene at the river is amazingly powerful and suggests that Kelithe finds a kind of peace that had previously eluded her. What is it about the river that allows her to find this peace? Discuss the river as a symbol of the power and the fury of motherhood. How does the water imagery in the novel shed light on the creative and destructive forces of women, which is such a central theme?

## A Conversation with Donna Hemans

Q. Where do you get the inspiration for your writing? How did you get the idea for this novel, for example? Is this based on any real-life events?

A. Inspiration for my writing comes from my life. For instance, the first chapter of *RIVER WOMAN* came from my memories of driving through Jamaica and witnessing women gathered at the riverside to wash. The heart of the story, too— a child left behind while a parent migrates—comes also from experience, though not my personal experience. When I began writing the novel, a friend was struggling with the difficult task of deciding whether her child should remain in Jamaica with relatives while she completed school and made better prepara-tions here, or whether her child should leave the comforts of a steady home life and join her struggles here. Each year became next year. And I began imagining the thousands of children across the Caribbean and the world who know their parents only by a photograph, a voice on the telephone, barrels of clothes and toys at Christmas. I wanted to write a novel about migration that didn't deal with the experience of immigrants in their new country but a story from the point of view of a child left behind.

Q. Similarly, are any of your characters inspired by the people in your life or do you truly pluck them from your imag-ination?

A. I try not to write directly about people I know. Even though the idea for RIVER WOMAN grew out of watching my friend's pain at not being able to be with her child, RIVER WOMAN is not her story. Certainly, when I write I think of people I know in order to create a believable character. In creating Grams, I imagined my grandmothers and grand-aunts, remembered the many occasions I saw them wearing old housedresses with safety pins holding the front of their dresses closed, remembered them at peace sitting on the verandah "ketching a little breeze," and their coded warnings via Jamaican proverbs like "When plantain want to die it shoot"; "What sweet nanny goat going run 'im belly." Timothy, too, is a combination of all my friends' children. One friend had a child who was singing and dancing as soon as she learned to talk. And Timothy does that—he turns everything into a song. Though I like to think that Kelithe is purely imaginative, perhaps her character incorporates some of the traits of some of the sad and needy girls I remember from high school.

Q. I couldn't help but be reminded of the question, "What happens to a dream deferred?" when reading your novel. Do you see disappointment and bitterness as main motivators for many of the characters in RIVER WOMAN?

A. There's some amount of bitterness in that the women of Standfast initially gloated when Kelithe returned from school pregnant. And the women were willing to do almost anything to ensure that Kelithe was punished for what they believed was a crime rather than be rewarded with a plane ticket. But I also think that Kelithe is simply a scapegoat. The town uses the death of the child to draw attention to what it lacks—running water, roads, electricity, attention from politicians and police.

Q. On page 214, the member of parliament realizes, as he watches the people of Standfast, that "he now understood the way poverty eroded pride." How you do you think poverty affects pride? Is this loss of pride inevitable? Do you consider the people of Standfast to be a proud people?

A. The member of parliament *thinks* he understands how poverty eroded pride. He believes the people of Standfast no longer have self-respect. But I think the people of Standfast remain proud. The people of Standfast are respectful of what they achieve despite the odds against them. Rather than wait for the politicians to fix the potholes, the people repair the road themselves. Also on page 214, Teacher Williams reminds himself to gather the men to repair the road. And on page 215, Maisey says that what the town needs is people who believe in themselves. I think poverty affects pride when people stop believing in themselves.

Q. The tension between younger and older generations plays a large role in your novel. Talk a little bit about the way you see the forces at work between younger women and older women. Do you think this tension is a good thing? Do you see it as a force of creation, or a force of destruction?

A. In *RIVER WOMAN*, the tension between the younger and older generations turns out to be a good thing. The younger generation was fighting the story of the town's failed potential, the myth that continues to hamper Standfast's growth. Toward the end of the novel, Teacher Williams observes the "charred remains of the bridge as a symbol of a promise now buried." It's his belief that once the weight of the failed promise is lifted, the town can emerge from stagnation. Ultimately the tension is a positive force because it leads to the roadblocks, which in turn pulls the politicians to the once-forgotten town. Sadly, Standfast receives attention at the expense of Kelithe.

Q. "Somewhere in all of this the truth was hidden, its heavy presence settling the way sediment does on the bottom of a river, to be uncovered only if the river goes dry or if a dredge is used to clean the riverbed." This is one of the final thoughts that Sonya has at the end of the novel regarding her grandson's death. Did Kelithe let Timothy die? Do you even know for sure? Is it necessary for the reader to know?

A. I want individual readers to decide for themselves whether Kelithe let Timothy die or if his drowning was simply an accident. In any situation, do we ever really know the absolute truth? No.

I believe, though, that the answer to what happened at the Rio Minho lies in what readers believe happens in the last chapter. Does Kelithe commit suicide when she walks into the river or does she simply walk into the water to relive her son's experience only to emerge and begin life anew? There are two things Kelithe has always wanted: to be a mother to her son without his experiencing life with a "soon-soon" promise, and to have a mother. At the end of the novel, Sonya has returned to New York and Kelithe is without son or mother. She doesn't have any of the things she craved.

If Kelithe does commit suicide, is her suicide a sign of guilt or despair? In answer to that, Kelithe's motivation throughout the novel remains constant, which I believe is a sign she is not guilty of watching her son drown. While the women of Standfast are initially adamant that Kelithe was responsible for Timothy's death, their focus shifts and in the end they are no longer concerned with the dead child but with the new promises of the politicians. Kelithe was simply a scapegoat. The MP promises a new life to Standfast, but no one can return to Kelithe what she has lost.

Q. This novel focuses pretty strongly on the idea of motherhood and the inherent sacrifice that comes along with a child. Do you consider this to be *the* central theme in your novel? Do you think that it is possible to have it all, to have children and not give up any of your dreams?

A. Motherhood is the central theme of the book. But I'm not yet a mother, so it's hard for me to say whether it is possible to have it all, children and viable dreams. Perhaps at a later stage in life I'll be better able to answer that question.

Q. Grams is an amazing character. To some extent she comes off as the hero of the story; the only character who maintains her own sense of right and wrong and her loyalty to her family. Did you envision Grams as the center of this novel? Is she indeed our hero?

A. I didn't think of Grams as the center of the novel, nor as the hero. Standfast, renewed by the new-found strength of the younger people of Standfast, emerges as the victor. Not only has the bridge that stood as a sign of the town's past failures been leveled, but the member of parliament has come to declare "a new life for Standfast." Though Grams is unwavering in her beliefs, the truth and Grams's strength of character are overshadowed by the townspeople's desire to see Standfast once again uplifted.

Q. Tell us a little about your writing process. Do you

suffer from writer's block? Do you have any interesting writing rituals?

A. I try to write in the mornings before I've become distracted by life itself. But I find that when I'm at my most creative—that is, when I'm excited by an idea or I've finally figured out how to complete a chapter or a short story—it's often difficult to sit still and work. I tend to cook or clean or walk from room to room, while ordering and reordering the words in my mind. To anyone peeping through my windows I probably look like a hyperactive child, sitting for a moment to type a sentence or two, walking a bit, checking a pot, cleaning a room, and returning to sit for another brief spell to add a little bit more.

Q. Do you have any projects that you are working on now? A second novel, perhaps?

A. I'm working on a second novel, tentatively titled *The Last Maroon*. It's the story of a seventeen-year-old Maroon girl who is sent from the Cockpit Country area of Jamaica to become a domestic helper for a middle-class family. The story is set in 1980 during a difficult political period in which over three hundred people were killed by politically motivated violence.